Fae and Moon Bound

Claimed Series Book 4

by

DOMINA ALEXANDRA

2023

Triplicity Publishing, LLC

ISBN-13: 978-1-970042-21-4
ISBN-10: 1-970042-21-4

Printed in the United States of America
First Edition – 2023
Cover Design: Triplicity Publishing, LLC
Interior Design: Triplicity Publishing, LLC
Editor: Julia Wagner - Triplicity Publishing, LLC

Also by Domina Alexandra

A Rogue's Redemption (Rogue Series book 1)

An Omega's Grief (Claimed Series book 3)

Endless as the Stars

Omega Rising (Claimed Series book 2)

I Belong With Her

A Night Claimed (Claimed Series book 1)

Love Undercover

Author's Notes

The tales of Bonnie and her pack. A werewolf that doesn't get a break from the things that lurk in the night. I have to admit, writing the Claimed Series leaves me with chills every time. The series was birthed from a real place. Mill City, Oregon is a small town and I have an amazing best friend who lives there. After my many trips to her home, I began to take Mill City in. The mountains, trees, and exclusion were captivating and scary at times. At night, there weren't streetlights, so it was dark, and I'd picture something predatory jumping out to get me.

And, one day I thought, "Wouldn't it be cool if werewolves lived here?" And the story was born.

I've been writing stories for years now and have yet to share my older work. Don't worry, I plan to. Writing for me came from years of being stuck in my head since I was such an introvert in my youth. I wrote poems, screenplays, and monologues, and soon discovered the excitement of writing longer stories. When I think of Bonnie now, as the main character in a very inclusive pack, I can't help but think of how much I always wanted a pack of my own. I've gotten that now with amazing friends like the one from Mill City, but it wasn't until I met Bonnie that I opened myself up to having a pack of my own.

Yes, I know the Claimed Series is a fantasy. But, is it really? Hmm.

If I can say one thing to all the readers, embrace your pack, find one, or even join mine! I thank you all for finding Bonnie! She's been going through it but she's learning. Aren't we all!

Thank you to Triplicity for giving me the platform to show my work. Your support is why I'm still with you! Thanks to my editor Julia Wagner, for not just editing but enjoying my stories! And to the entire team that helped design the cover and turn a story into one everyone will read.

I would like to dedicate this book to Mill City, Oregon. It wasn't until this book that I began to see how much I love your town with its streams, mountains, and trees. Even the cougars…of for this book werewolves!

And to my best friend, Tessa, for living there and entertaining my ideas of werewolves living near her. I promise not to let vampires stay too long. They might be coming…

Chapter One

Frozen by muddled thoughts, I lay quietly, trapped between what was reality and what was my past resurfacing. Her fingers were soft, grazing down the curve of my jaw. There were many things I loved about her. Regret squeezed my lungs shut, the fear of never being able to tell her I loved her again. Not saying yes, when she whispered in my ear to marry her as I slept.

"My Collins. It has been too long." There was that consoling soft whisper in my ears again. It had haunted my dreams for years. Tainted any chance at finding love again. Not until…

The light came to me from lucid dreams. My brows pinched together as my head swayed from side to side. My eyes fluttered open, the light causing me to squint. Tears stained my cheeks. My mouth was dry and pasty from lack of water. I tried to lick my lips and the taste was bitter to my tongue.

I used my nose to smell where I was, finding nothing familiar. It took my eyes a minute to adjust, and I stared up at the rough interior of the ceiling, carvings of patterns I could not recognize from any modern décor.

My instinct to run and find my mate nearly heaved me forward but I sucked in a breath instead. I squeezed my eyes closed to let go of my urgency to shift. Heat swarmed my belly and it raised to my chest, my wolf announcing itself.

Calm. I spoke to my wolf, soothing it. This was different. I'd never been able to talk to my wolf this way. I could feel my Omega grin, pleased that I had easily reached out without the struggle I normally had. In the midst of fear, I had gained a new insight by letting go of my human need to be in control. My wolf was me. And now I was awake and aware of my surroundings, and my wolf was awake with me.

When I opened my eyes again the bed dipped, and a hand pressed against my forearm. I was not naïve. This wasn't my pack's home, and this touch didn't belong to my mate. It was her. The woman who had haunted my dreams for the past week and the woman who had once stolen my heart were one in the same.

Alexis leaned over my body like a lover soothing me awake. Her brown eyes widened when our eyes locked, excited to see me. I expected to feel cold rough fingers, but Alexis's were warm and soothing, despite the darkness she contained.

I shuddered when the tips of Alexis's fingers brushed over the spot where I'd been stabbed. I grimaced, reliving the dagger that pierced through me. The reptilian vympyrus, Jaleel, had enjoyed hearing me scream out in pain. The silver blade seared through me, and time seemed to slow before darkening.

I had willingly given myself up to Jaleel after he'd enthralled and kidnapped my brother, Darnell as a successful tactic to force my decision. My brother and I weren't close and the knowledge of him being my nephew and him knowing the truth about where I'd come from long before I, had only made my reunion with him more difficult. But he was family and I loved him despite his flaws. I could not let my brother or anyone else be under Alexis's control.

I wanted to pretend Alexis had been only in my dreams but seeing her now, it was a reality check I could not change. Mahogany brown hair fell over her oval face. One corner of her mouth lifted into a grin when our eyes locked for a second time. Her beautifully light brown skin hadn't aged.

I laid on the bed, my gaze never drifting from Alexis. She wore the same face as someone I once knew. She repositioned, giving me room to sit up. Expression blissful and warm, Alexis only watched me with anticipation. Her lips curved into a smile, expecting me to reciprocate her feelings.

Even if I closed my eyes again, it would not change the outcome. No. I couldn't hide from this. I scooted upright, still a little weak. I needed food if I was going to recover completely. I wore only a sports bra; there was no sign of injury when I brushed my fingers over my stomach. Being a werewolf had its rewards and fast healing was one to be thankful for. I stared down at myself; no residue of proof of being stabbed.

My eyes peered around, guarded, and unsure of what was happening. I decided to focus my attention on everything but Alexis. I was on top of silk crimson sheets. The walls were painted a dark maroon with gold feather designs. There were candles meticulously placed at the center of both nightstands alongside the bed, calmly lighting the room.

I kept my head down.

"Where is my sister?" I asked. The last thing I remembered after Jaleel had stabbed me was my sister carrying me. I knew she was here.

When I looked up at Alexis, there was no intake of breath or heartbeat to alert me of what she was feeling. I glanced up briefly and gazed at the vein in her neck that carried no pulse. Alexis was dead, or what the supernatural word referred to as *undead.* Afraid to meet her eyes, I shifted my head back to the sheets and waited for her response.

"Is that all you have to say?" Alexis asked, dismayed by my standoffish demeanor.

My hands pressed to the sides of my body and gripped the sheets tightly. Carefully, I let out a breath to control my wolf's potential temper. I didn't want to be here, and Alexis was a fool to think that I did.

How did she expect me to respond? I was hurt and tried not to show it, but I could never hide my emotions from her.

"I have nothing to say to you until I see my sister." I could barely control my tone; my larynx was suffocating from indignation. I did what I could to control my agony, but the hurt came out.

Alexis moved off the bed with inhuman speed and stood beside the door, arm stretched out in invitation for me to leave.

"I'll take you to her now." She couldn't hide her frustration, lips pursed, jaw tightening.

I slid off the bed and searched for my shirt, finding it folded on the dresser across the room. My body ached. My ribs were damaged and still healing from the stab wound. I dressed and ignored her eyes on my body. I lingered near the dresser and a brief glance at her was all it took to weaken my brave demeanor.

Alexis turned and walked out of the room. I slid my shirt over my head, frantic to see that my sister was unharmed. She guided me through a long corridor made of smoothly carved stone, the curved ceiling shaped like a wide *U*. There were taper candles every twelve feet to keep the ambiance softly lit. The surface was made of stone, no wind to hint that we were close to an exit. I couldn't smell trees or wild animals and I furrowed my brow, realizing there was no way Rikki would be able to find me and come here without a fight.

We reached a spiral staircase. I peered down, tilting my body awkwardly on my tiptoes to get a look as to where we were heading.

Alexis noticed what I was doing and stopped on the third step.

"You aren't going to reach her that way." She sounded amused. Alexis didn't bother turning to face me and continued down the stairs. I tried not to notice the tightly fitted leather pants she wore that hugged her ass.

I shook my head and focused on the obvious. I was in Alexis's safe place, so this had to be the cave I'd come to when the black witches had given me the blood spell. I'd met my biological father and the urgency to meet him had left me with only more questions.

At the bottom was a short passage. I was about to question if she was lying about having my sister but as we rounded the corner, I could smell my sister's anxiety. I walked into a cavernous hall; a dining table made of stone was at the center of the open space with oak wood chairs around it.

Wood through the chest could kill a vampire. Either Alexis's sense of humor or lack of fear made me stare at wood chairs. It was like werewolves sitting with a silver sword in the hand of an enemy. A glass chandelier draped over the dining table with candles replacing what would normally be lightbulbs. Decorative vintage art hung on the walls, changing the dark and dull ambiance into a warm and inviting living space.

My sister stood when I came into view.

"Bonnie!" Braelin's posture straightened, relieved to see me. She was seated in one of the chairs. She sneered at Jaleel, who lingered a little too close to her for my comfort.

I rushed to Braelin's side and noticed her wrists were bound by silver cuffs. Other than being limited in movement, Braelin didn't appear to be in any pain.

"He hasn't touched you in any way?" My gaze drifted up to Jaleel for a second, but he didn't pay attention to me.

"I am fine. Did she touch you?" Braelin asked, glaring at Alexis, her hatred not going unnoticed.

"I just woke up." I cupped Braelin's cheek and pressed my forehead against hers in regret. "You shouldn't have come." If anything happened to Braelin, the pain wouldn't be something I'd ever get over. I wasn't as strong as Jaleel, but I'd find a way to kill him if he touched her. That was a promise I'd keep to myself.

Braelin's brow furrowed. "I was not going to let you leave without me."

"Now that you can see she is fine—" Alexis started.

"Uncuff her!" I turned, fists bawled tightly, my gold eyes glaring into Alexis's brown ones. I had not forgotten the eyes that taunted me in my dreams. Alexis was trying to appear human to me.

"We both know you have too many servants throughout this maze-like cave," I said. "It would be pointless for her to attack you head on or try to escape. And she won't try to leave without me."

Alexis stood unmoving and quiet. Her mouth curved upward, eyes flashing black with constricted sapphire pupils.

"Acknowledge me and perhaps I will consider," she said. Clearly, Alexis was tired of being dismissed.

I grimaced and before I could lift my head up, tears welled in my eyes. I sucked in a shuddering breath and felt my lips quiver as I blew out slowly. My jaw trembled with rage, and I let out another frustrated breath.

If I acknowledged Alexis, it would mean that she was real. Something I was not ready to do. I looked at my sister before deciding. Braelin's wrists showed what were close to third degree burns; her skin was peeling and inflamed from the silver cuffs. The longer they stayed latched to her wrists, the worse it would get. I knew Braelin could manage but that was not the point. Braelin shouldn't have to suffer in the slightest because of me.

When I finally looked up at Alexis, a tear slid down my cheek. I wasn't scared. I was hurt and didn't know how to release it without screaming. Alexis was as beautiful as I'd remembered. Chestnut eyes, long dark hair that I'd get lost in while twirling it around my fingers. I never thought I'd see her again. Her lightly creamed brown skin still looked as smooth and soft as I remembered. Everything about her was the same, from her petite body to her full lips. She was stunning and I hated her for it. She oozed confidence that I always inspired to have. A black woman who knew how to stand on her own two feet, comfortable in her skin and open to possibilities. That's one of the reasons that drew me to her.

"What's wrong?" Braelin noticed my hesitation and dread in confronting Alexis, as if the tears hadn't been obvious enough. "Bonnie," she muttered, and I glanced briefly at my sister long enough for her to see the truth. Her mouth hung open, shifting a glance toward Alexis before speaking to me. "You know her?" she said it as if I'd always known who had been causing trouble for our pack.

"Much longer than you've known her," Alexis said proudly. She took a step in my direction but halted when we locked eyes.

I lifted my hand, shoulders tense. I wouldn't let Alexis act like things between us were rainbows and sunshine.

"Is it Alexis or is it…Rachelle?" I asked, not sure if I ever knew her. Evidently, we were going to have this conversation.

Alexis pursed her lips, no longer smiling. "Both!" she responded, sounding indifferent, and nodded for Jaleel to give us some distance. "I never lied—"

"Shut up!" I spat, frustrated and irate. My body trembled, my wolf on the verge of taking over if I didn't calm down. Alexis moved closer. I shot up faster than she expected and took a quick step back, holding my hand up high enough to align with her face. "I swear…come near me and I'll punch you so hard that you might actually feel something." More tears threatened to spill but I held it in long enough to say my next words. "Was I always blind to what you are, or did you have a sudden life-altering change that forced you to leave me?"

Alexis showed genuine human emotion for the first time since I woke up. Not arrogance. There was regret. Her eyes softened and she tried her best not to say the wrong thing.

"Yes and no," she confessed. I could see regret spreading past her eyes and seeping down to her fidgeting fingers. "I have always been this way, but I did not leave willingly."

I snorted and wanted to say something harsh.

"You are telling me the almighty vampire witch was forced to leave behind the one person she claimed to love?" I said, doubtful. I ran both my hands through my hair, suddenly in need of fresh air. I had so much rage building inside me that it could devour this entire cave. "What kind of monster are you?" I hissed.

"Don't call me that!" Alexis took another step, and I froze. "My love for you was always real." She closed the distance between us and carefully reached out to touch my face. Her fingertips brushed my cheek, mouth agape as a crimson tear slid down the side of her face. There was remorse in her eyes. "I had no choice. Things were much more complicated back then."

I was trapped by her gaze and the softness of her fingers caressing my cheek. She wasn't enthralling me. It was our past that trapped me.

"Leave her alone!" Braelin snarled, trying to reach me but unable.

I moved my face away, taking another step back. I expected Alexis to move toward me again, but she stood immobile. Her eyes shifted to the floor; I could feel pain emanating from her. How could she be the one hurting? I would not feel sorry for her.

"I am not a monster." Though her tone was calm I could tell I cracked an emotion out of her, that even she didn't want to acknowledge.

I decided not to poke a sensitive issue and thought of a memory we once shared. Alexis had never been someone who liked to be called crazy and despite everything, I wouldn't throw that in her face now.

"I'm sorry." The words slipped out of my mouth before I could stop myself.

Braelin let out a gasp, shocked by my apology.

I hated this already. In less than ten minutes I was already apologizing to the woman I was ready to fight before I woke up. I hadn't seen this coming. But how was I supposed to pretend a couple years of my life didn't circle around Alexis once. But for me, she was Rachelle.

"Bonnie, please tell me what's going on?" Braelin wasn't naive.

Alexis walked toward my sister, and I moved to the other side of Braelin, watchful of Alexis as she released my sister from the cuffs.

Alexis bowed her head and smiled. "I will give you two a moment. But I expect a private conversation with you after."

I nodded. I was tempted to say thank you, but I sucked in a breath instead. At the end of the day, Alexis had forced my hand into coming here by threatening everyone I loved. She wasn't the good person in this story, despite our history.

Braelin opened her mouth to speak but I lifted my finger to my lips, signaling for her to stay silent. I wanted to make sure we were completely alone before we started to talk. I could no longer sense Alexis's presence, and my shoulders loosened.

"What's going on?" Braelin grumbled, rubbing her wrists which were already healing.

I moved toward the table and took a seat, all energy leaving me. I wondered about that same question too. For the past five years I'd been living with the acceptance of never seeing Rachelle again and here she was now as a black witch and a vampire named Alexis.

"She..." I was stuck in memory. Braelin tapped my hand and drew attention back to her, and I frowned. "She was the woman I thought I'd never see again."

"Okay, now you're being vague," Braelin huffed and took a seat, facing me.

"I knew her as Rachelle," I explained.

Braelin shrugged. I realized I had never mentioned Rachelle to anyone except Rikki, and that was recent. Even then, I never uttered her name. I had wanted to bring up Rachelle, but it would only bring back the pain and sadness I'd felt and tried to release years ago. I never got over Rachelle and instead accepted that I might not see her again.

"Rachelle was my girlfriend." I frowned, rephrasing my words. "She was my fiancée. She'd proposed and I asked for time. But I was planning to say yes."

When my eyes locked onto Braelin's, there was an unsettling glare that told me she clearly did not approve. She craned her neck to one side and nodded before speaking.

"Okay! I didn't see that coming." I heard Braelin's jaw pop, and I knew if I didn't explain soon, the next time Alexis came in here Braelin was going to lunge.

"She wasn't like this though." I would have never fallen in love with someone who took pleasure in hurting others. Alexis played mind games and enjoyed creating chaos. Rachelle was nurturing and lively. "Rachelle was sweet, funny, and very human like. I don't remember or think she ever acted in a way that would suggest otherwise. I mean, I didn't go checking her pulse to see if she was alive, but still."

Braelin stood up, needing space to think. "You don't care for her still, do you?"

I cleared my throat, not anticipating that question. I didn't want my sister doubting who I wanted to stand beside me.

"Braelin. I am happy with Rikki and would never consider anyone else."

"She isn't anyone else," Braelin reminded me. "She was a woman you clearly loved and by the simple fact that you aren't behaving how you normally would around a threat, it leaves me to wonder."

"And how would I normally act?" I argued, defensively.

Braelin snarled. "For starters, not apologetic for hurting her damn feelings."

"Rachelle can be sensitive to certain—"

"Rachelle," Braelin argued, her eyes a dark gold. "Her name is Alexis. The same Alexis who has been stalking you. Sent ghouls and got a reptilian vympyrus to take you. Killed innocent people."

I nodded. "You're right. Alexis did all of that. And Alexis is Rachelle. I know that."

"And you didn't answer my question!" Braelin said. She sighed, sitting back beside me and taking a slow breath. "You can't still care for her?"

Braelin's inquisitive gaze told me my response mattered. I didn't know how to answer the question. It wasn't like Rachelle ran off with another woman or broke my heart. I thought she'd been kidnapped or worse. I'd been happy and ready to marry her before she disappeared. I couldn't answer my sister and kept my eyes averted.

Braelin sighed, leaning back into the chair.

Changing the subject, she asked, "How is she up? I thought she was in some state of hibernation and only able to reach you subconsciously." Braelin looked me over, searching for bite marks. "Or was that the illusion she gave?"

I brushed my fingers over my neck, feeling nothing but the scar I received when the ghoul bit me.

"Or perhaps, it was your assumption." Alexis stood under the archway that led to a different passage, a glass of blood in her hands.

"Then how are you awake?" Braelin questioned, standing protectively in front of me.

Alexis smiled, finding Braelin amusing. "Synthetic blood from your bloodline. I have merely been bound here, not unconscious."

"What do you mean?" I asked. Braelin and I stood, not comfortable having our backs to Alexis. There was no point in Braelin attempting to shield me. If Alexis wanted to come near me, she was more than capable.

"You have been given time with your sister. Don't I deserve the same courtesy after so much time apart?" Alexis asked, eyes lingering on me like a lover ready to be reunited.

I dropped my eyes, conflicted by how I should act around her. I knew Braelin was right. My past with Alexis made it hard for me to put a huge wall up between us, but she had answers I needed to know. And the love we shared had been special and not something easily forgotten.

"I'm not leaving—" Braelin's eyes went wide as her mouth shut forcefully from Alexis's magic. Her hands rushed up to her mouth and nose, bumping into the chair. The muscles in her neck strained and I moved to see what was wrong, realizing Braelin was unable to breathe.

"Whatever you are doing, stop!" I screamed at Alexis, who had her attention strictly on my sister. Rushing over to Alexis, I stepped in front of her, blocking her view.

Her eyes darted at me and whatever magic that possessed my sister released her.

"You don't want me to call you a monster and yet you act like one," I pointed out.

Alexis's eyes beamed with rage, her stance straight and demanding. For a long moment, neither of us spoke as I listened to my sister regain her composure.

Not shifting a glance, Alexis called out a name. "Jaleel."

The reptilian vympyrus stepped into view on command. "Yes, sire."

"Take the werewolf," Alexis ordered.

My eyes widened.

Alexis took a seat, placing her glass on the table.

"She will not be harmed as long as she does not resist," Alexis assured me.

Braelin stood firm and guarded. "I'm not going to leave you with her."

"I will be fine. But you won't if you fight them on this," I said.

Alexis wore a smug grin. "Yes. I am more than capable of keeping her safe. More than your Alpha can."

"Don't insult my mate. That's the quickest way to stop me from acknowledging you." I had no intention of hearing Alexis bad-mouth Rikki or anyone I care about. I shut my eyes and blew out slowly. "Please Braelin. Go." I wasn't asking her as a sister but as an Alpha's mate.

Braelin sneered, eyes narrowed on Alexis before she nodded once and was guided out by Jaleel.

Alexis sat with her legs crossed and eyes closed, consuming the rest of the blood in her glass. When she was finished, she placed the glass on the table and licked her lips.

I stood, guarded both physically and emotionally. I struggled not to forget that she was the vampire witch who had brought harm to my pack and allies. But all I could do was stare at her, nauseated and bewildered. Alexis tried to pretend my reaction to her wasn't valid or reasonable, but I could see through her stiff posturing she carried regret and sorrow.

It had been five years and the way I had felt about her wasn't mild or fleeting. It was a wound I had placed a big Band-Aid over when it should have healed with gentle care. When she looked at me, for a heartbeat I saw the woman I fell in love with, and I needed to shut my eyes. I couldn't see the vampire witch that Braelin wanted me to hate.

"Not happy to see me?" Alexis whispered.

I sucked in a breath, baffled by her question. My jaw popped and I knew that was my wolf ready to shift.

"Are you serious?" There had to be some part of Alexis that knew what she had done was wrong. A tear managed to slip out and I quickly wiped it away, not wanting to cry in front of her. It wasn't about weakness. I had no intention of allowing her to think my tears were for her to console. "You just opened me up completely and tore my heart out. Which part of your freaking mind has this delusion that I'd be happy to see you?"

Alexis sneered and shook her head as if not interested in hearing my grievance.

"You lived well, I see!" she muttered.

I snorted, mystified by her reaction. My fingers dug into my hips, staring at her in consternation.

"Will you stop with this...facade?" I moved my hand up quickly, gesturing for her not to speak as her mouth opened. She was quick to defend herself without taking the time to listen. If there was one thing I was good at when it came to our relationship, it was making Alexis see beyond her own bullshit.

"You're acting detached. As if I have no right to want to punch, scream or fucking..." I bit my tongue, wanting to let my wolf out and kill something. I wasn't violent but she was bringing that part of me out. I couldn't let her have that power over me, but she did. I let out a growl and shook my head frantically. So much time wasted on thinking she'd been kidnapped and murdered. At that time in my life, I'd been deemed broken by my own thoughts. My emotions were scattered, seeing her standing before me now.

"I can't believe you." I squeezed my eyes shut, my head spinning out of control. There was so much I wanted to say but nothing could come from my muddled thoughts. "You tried to kill people that I loved."

"I didn't try anything!" Alexis sneered. "I sent ghouls after you, yes. But if I wanted your pack or Alpha dead, they would be."

"She's my mate," I reminded her. Alexis didn't reply and I rolled my eyes. "What about the humans? Or taking my brother?" I questioned.

Alexis nodded. "That was Jaleel being a bit too ambitious. Once I found out about him taking your brother, I told him to bring him back to you. And he did...unharmed!"

She was unbelievable. Alexis had an excuse for everything.

"I have never lied to you," she stated. She spoke quickly, spotting my reaction. "I never shared the truth of what I was...but I never stated a lie." Alexis stood, leaving her glass on the table. "Therefore, I am not lying to you now."

Alexis closed the distance between us, giving me one of her famous smiles I used to adore. I shut my eyes, not wanting to fall for that trick.

"I have a right to be upset," I said. Part of me wanted to find the women I knew and had searched months for. But, thinking about Rikki, I wouldn't mislead Alexis into thinking my heart was open for her to snake her way in. She was dangerous and a threat to everyone I cared about. That was a fact I needed to remind myself of.

"I may not like it, but I won't disagree," Alexis replied.

I opened my eyes to find her seated back at the table. She was staring down at her empty glass. I hadn't even felt or heard her walk away from me. "I understand your bitterness towards seeing me. And I acknowledge that our reunion wasn't under the best approach." Her eyes shifted my way as she spoke. "I even admit that I am not the same woman you fell in love with. I have done terrible things."

"Like keep my father prisoner?" I stated. I wasn't sure if she knew that I'd met him recently when searching for clues to who was stalking me. After meeting the witch coven, High Priestess Mira and being spelled to slip into an astral plane, I'd nearly fallen off a cliff and been rescued by a man I never thought I'd meet.

Alexis nodded. "Your father knows exactly why he is bound to me."

"Should there ever be a reason?" I retorted.

"In this world, yes!" Alexis stated. "I never wanted you to see this side of life, where things lurk in the dark, but you're here. And this is the reality of the supernatural world. Debts must be paid, and it can be done in many forms."

A thought came to mind. "You knew who I was when we first met!" I accused. "Sought me out."

Alexis stood again. "You must be hungry." As if telepathically called, Jaleel walked into the open space.

I pursed my lips, annoyed by her ignoring my question.

"Why am I here? Clearly, you don't need my blood," I waved my hand toward her empty glass. Alexis continued to ignore me. "Rachelle!" I finally snapped, using the name I knew her by.

Her eyes darted to me, and Jaleel stood in anticipation of what his master might do. Alexis turned to face me. "It is too soon for me to answer those questions. Because those questions will lead to more you are not ready to know." I frowned as she continued. "I want you to trust me. At least, the version you once loved." I averted my eyes, not sure what to say. "Or perhaps...some part of you still loves," she added.

This time I narrowed my eyes at her. "I only want the truth."

"What is that saying?" Alexis thought for a moment. She tilted her head, grasping for the word that couldn't form in her mind.

Jaleel grinned in reply. "She can't handle the truth," he slurred.

Alexis grinned. "Exactly." She walked up to me and reached for my hand, but I pulled away. Her expression went blank. "If you think me impossible to understand or harsh, then fine. I have lived too many centuries and had to be this way to survive. But you will care for me again because you will see that I still love you. Despite your disdain in how I *claimed* you, I have no doubt you will understand that I did this for you."

Alexis looked at Jaleel and he sneered, looking at me.

"My apologies for manipulating your human nephew."

I snorted, seeing that he was very much *up to date* on my family's dynamics in referring to my brother as being my nephew.

Alexis lifted her chin and Jaleel continued.

"And for stabbing you. I was only making a point," he clarified.

"What point was that? How much you like sticking daggers into others or that you like brainwashing innocent people?"

Jaleel didn't like my response. He looked ready to say something, but Alexis interjected.

"Perhaps you'd like to see your sister. The feast will be in one hour."

"Feast?" I questioned.

Alexis smiled and before I could ask more questions, she was gone, moving at a speed I barely captured.

Jaleel stood watchful of me. "This way!"

Arms crossed over my chest; I took a moment to get over my own anger. There was no point complaining to Jaleel or trying to find Alexis. I needed to be patient, something I always struggled with but liked to think I'd gotten better at.

Jaleel was unbothered by my emotions, waiting for me to follow.

When I sighed, that was the signal he needed to know I was ready. I rolled my eyes, knowing I wasn't done asking questions. Alexis would tell me what I wanted. It was only a matter of time.

Chapter Two

After walking up what felt like several flights of stone stairs, Jaleel opened the wooden door, and a gust of wind blew through my unkempt hair. The two braids I had needed a makeover but that was the last thing on my mind.

Braelin stood from the chair, rushing to my side as Jaleel slammed the door shut. There was an opening that exposed the nighttime outdoor atmosphere but from the distant trees and mountains, I could tell we were too high to climb down or up. We could jump from a greater distance than any human could but after a few hundred feet, our risk of splattering was greater than landing on our feet. It was the perfect caged room. The only furnishings were a full-size mattress on the floor and a chair pressed into the corner of the wall at the opposite end. The open ambiance that led outside of the cave looked like a perfect place to sightsee if we were willing guests, taking a tour, versus prisoners.

"Are you okay?" Braelin asked. She managed to scan my body like a bite detector without hovering too close like she normally did.

I nodded. "Yeah," I lied. Inside, I was freaking out. I had pretended to be strong when I first saw Alexis, but my insides had crumbled and melted all at once when I realized who it was. After all this time, Alexis had been alive and well. Or Rachelle. Part of me didn't know which name to use.

"No, you're not," Braelin said softly. She sighed and pulled me into a hug.

I didn't want to be comforted, feeling guilty. I'd brought trouble to our pack again. But as Braelin's arms curled around me, I couldn't stop myself from crying. There was so much pain bottled inside me in such a brief time. And most of all, I missed my mate. I hated the torture Rikki was under, knowing I was the cause. Our relationship had finally reached a point of deeper understanding and I'd been excited to explore more of it. I hadn't seen this setback coming.

"We will get back to your mate!" Braelin promised. "Just work on your meditations. I know that is the key."

I nodded and pulled away. Braelin reached out, wiping my tears away.

"Thank you."

She smiled. "I always got you. That's what sisters are for."

I nodded.

"I should not have given you a tough time. I can see this is difficult for you. And it's clear you two have history." Braelin guided me toward the open space, the dark sky not hindering us from admiring the distant ocean of trees and mountains. "What did she say?"

"Not much," I grumbled, slouching from emotional exhaustion. I shut my eyes, trying to retrace the conversation between Alexis and me. "The most I got was...she's doing this for me." I wanted to laugh but didn't have it in me to try. Besides, I'd only end up crying.

"Why put on a performance to scare you if she cares about you?" Braelin frowned, not believing that.

I shook my head. "I don't know."

"She could have just come and asked nicely to work together to keep you safe if that's the case," Braelin said, trying to figure it out. "But she chose to stalk and harass you. Killed innocent humans. The ghouls, everything."

"I know," I sighed, not wanting to be reminded of everything. "I questioned her on that and though she admits to a few things, she stated Jaleel went too far without asking permission." Braelin's expression darkened. I reached over and patted her arm. "I know you don't, but I believe her. She has never openly lied to me."

"Bonnie!" Braelin's disapproval was obvious.

"I'm not saying she's innocent of anything or trying to defend her. I am aware that time has passed between us, but I must believe that the woman I loved is still in there and wouldn't lie directly to my face," I said.

Braelin inhaled, letting out a long breath.

"Okay," she accepted. She took a moment to breathe in the fresh air. Who knew when we'd get a chance like this again?

Braelin spoke again, wary not to push. "But can you at least admit to yourself that part of you might be blinded by your past?"

I opened my mouth to argue but Braelin gave me an expression that shut it.

"I'm not shaming you for whatever you might have felt for her," Braelin reassured me. "I know you wouldn't have been with her if she didn't have some good in her. But clearly things have changed." I knew Braelin was right.

"What I'm saying is...feelings that are left unanswered don't go away that easily. And she left you with a lot of unanswered questions. She left you longing for her. I know you love Rikki and would never do anything to jeopardize your relationship intentionally. But if you keep trying to convince yourself that your love for her no longer exists, you will make a mistake."

I stared off into the trees, watching snowflakes begin to float from the sky. It was Thanksgiving by now. My mom and brother had to be out of their minds, and Rikki was probably trying to pretend she was okay and help them. I trusted my pack and knew they'd be there for Rikki too.

My biological father had told me not to resist. And I was beginning to think he wasn't talking about resisting her compulsion or desire to feed from me. He'd known my connection to Alexis.

I needed to feel my emotions, the good and the bad, and not pretend or ignore them. It would be the only way I could finally move on completely. Part of me wondered if that was why I was so resistant to being mated to Rikki in the first place. Not just that I was introduced to a new world but that I was afraid of loving Rikki only to lose her. And I was still unsettled by the loss of Rachelle.

"I hear you," I finally replied.

Braelin looked toward the door and pressed her index finger against her lips. She was exceptionally good at using her nose on a consistent basis, where I struggled to remember I had one. We sat quietly, Braelin repositioning to face the door when someone knocked a few seconds later.

Whoever it was, they had manners. Jaleel would have burst in, if only to agitate me.

When no one opened the door, Braelin spoke, "Come in." She chuckled softly, clearly thinking the same thing as me.

I wasn't sure if I should say thank you for knocking and make a potential friend to utilize when the time came.

A woman stepped into view; a soft smile displayed across her face. She was a dark-skinned woman in her early twenties with short curly hair and curvy build.

"My sire requests your presence at the dining hall," she said to us both.

I thought it would be smart to use my nose. There was no way an innocent looking woman could be here willingly. She seemed relaxed and at home. I casually took a breath and was met with the worst odor I'd smelled since I once picked up a patient with a stage four decubitus ulcer. And that odor was unforgettable. I recognized the younger woman's scent and suddenly had the urge to take a step back.

The younger woman's grin widened, suspecting I'd figured out what she was. She looked amused.

"You can call me Arlana. And yes, I am the sophisticated and consciously awake version of a ghoul. Not like the ghouls you have dealt with. Mindless and incompetent." Her full smile lasted a few seconds longer than I liked and I shifted my gaze everywhere but on her.

I could feel her eyes on me, and it did not make me feel comfortable.

Braelin broke the tension, shifting Arlana's attention to her with a question.

"This feast doesn't require us as sacrificial meals, does it?" Braelin asked with a tolerant expression.

I smacked her over the arm, not finding her joke funny.

Arlana laughed, amused by my sister, and gave a response I preferred not to hear.

"As long as our current meal doesn't run away, no." Arlana's eyes shifted thoroughly over Braelin's body like a dessert on a plate.

If Braelin heard the threat behind Arlana's tone, she pretended not to notice.

"Well, I already have one person attempting to take a bite out of me, so you'll have to get in line."

I stood, impressed by how level-headed Braelin appeared as if unaffected by the ghoul's presence. Braelin lived with an unwillingness to be afraid or intimidated by anyone, and that I admired. The only time I ever saw fear in her eyes was when I was in danger. The love and loyalty she had for me were strong and unwavering, and I aspired to be more like her every day.

"Please follow." Arlana dropped the conversation and turned away.

Braelin reached for my hand as we followed Arlana from a safe distance. I pictured us as kids, Braelin holding my hand and walking me home from school and I smiled. Darnell and my other brother Devon never gave me memories like that. I sighed, leaving my thoughts behind. Devon was in the military, but for most of my life, he'd always been the emotionally unavailable brother. It was never personal. He simply didn't have the emotional compacity to acknowledge other people's feelings.

We arrived at an unfamiliar part of the cave in which candles of various shapes were outlined along the walls. The ambiance was creatively decorative, instantly reminding me of the time Rachelle decorated our home when we first moved in together. She loved a mixture of bright colors with art and antique items to fill the open space.

When my eyes found Alexis sitting at the long carved wooden table, I wondered what happened to the woman I'd planned to spend the rest of my life with. She looked the same. Beautiful straight shoulder length hair that never looked unkempt with the biggest brown eyes you could fall for.

Alexis wore a long satin V-neck dress with an open back and double slit. Her long smooth legs were crossed and exposed, and I swallowed what felt like my lungs, suddenly forgetting how to breathe. Her smile could make the strongest hearts fall to their knees. She stood, walking up to me as if I was the only one in the room.

"I do have clothes that you would look exquisite in, but I know you well enough to not bother offering them to you at this time."

I smiled weakly and nodded. The best way to overcome her was to feel my emotions and move past them. I knew this and yet I felt uncertain of what to do. I loved Rikki and all I could think about was getting home to her and my pack. Hell, I even missed Lloyd though I'd never tell him. But I was here, and the only way back was through Alexis and our past.

"What are we doing here?" Braelin asked, keeping close to my side.

Alexis treated my sister like an intrusive guest by not responding but gave a brief icy glare before softening her expression.

"I made your favorite." Alexis pulled out a chair for me right beside where she sat.

There was a softness in her voice, and I stared, unsure of her intention. I didn't want to over-think any action or statement Alexis made. The best I could hope for was to convince her to let us go. I took the seat she offered. My sister sat herself next to me, taking Alexis's seat.

The shiny gold platters were topped with silver plastic coverings that concealed the food. The silk tablecloth was gold and white, with flower patterns as the landscape. Alexis moved around the table, lighting an extra candle which she placed at the center.

"I prepared this myself. So please forgive me in advance if it isn't quite how you remember." Alexis was treating this evening like a date, despite my sister's presence. "Slow cooked roast beef with double baked potatoes and sauteed asparagus and cornbread." She grinned, pleased with herself as she unveiled the food.

"You cooked this?" Braelin gestured toward the food, doubtful.

Alexis ignored my sister's question. She was doing an exceptional job pretending Braelin didn't exist.

I tapped Braelin's thigh and gave her a wide look. There was no point in antagonizing Alexis when it would only hurt us in the end.

Taking the initiative, I smiled politely. "It smells great. You forgot one thing," I pointed out.

Alexis's grin brightened. "No! I would never forget the best part." With speed I couldn't catch, she left and was back within a few seconds, holding a bottle of merlot.

Naturally, remembering the dinners Alexis would cook for me, I felt compelled to laugh.

"Wow. I can't see Jaleel going out to a store to buy that," I said.

I could feel Braelin's intense eyes burning into the side of my face. She thought I was already falling under Alexis's spell.

Despite how much time passed between us, instincts told me Alexis would never spell or compel me to fall in love with her again. The one thing I remembered most about our love was her need to feel equally loved in the purest way. I would always have love for Alexis, but I knew where my heart belonged. I needed Braelin to trust me.

Alexis took a seat at the head of the table as the ghoul that had assisted us into the dining hall brought in an additional plate. Alexis watched me until I looked to her for an explanation.

"I wanted to do something nice for you."

"Okay," I softly replied. My manners went out the window when my nose got too close to the meat, and I dug in. I hadn't eaten, and it would help me regain my strength. I took a bite of the meat and my sister stared at me dumbfounded.

"What?" I asked.

I pointed my nose to the sound of footsteps coming our way, but Braelin had stood before I realized who it was. When he walked around the corner into the open, tears flooded my eyes. Not necessarily for me but for Braelin.

I could feel her anxiety and anger mixing like a bad chemical reaction ready to erupt. Braelin moved toward our father but was looking directly at Alexis when she spoke.

"You call this being nice? Allowing us to see our father."

Malcolm stood, shocked and terrified to see us. He hadn't known we were here. His eyes filled with tears but despite the eagerness to rush into Braelin's arms, his feet were glued to the floor. He looked at Alexis, and she nodded. He moved frantically around the table, closing the distance between them.

Braelin cried in our father's arms as I sat awkwardly but happy for her. She'd missed him fiercely and I knew part of her couldn't believe he was alive until she saw him for herself.

I glanced at Alexis as she'd been watching me.

"I called him out here for you. Greet your father if you like."

I frowned, averting my eyes. There was part of me that wanted to get up and do exactly that, but I didn't know him at the end of the day. And most of that was Alexis's fault. I finished my plate and waved for her to open the bottle of wine. Alexis only smirked and opened it, pouring me a drink.

"Stop acting like some hero," Braelin snapped.

Alexis paused and placed the wine bottle on the table.

Braelin stood in a posture that suggested she could shift at any moment. Malcolm reached for his daughter's hand in a plea for her to be silent. Braelin's fingernails were replaced with claws, overwhelmed by seeing our father and Alexis's constant dismissal.

"Malcolm. Sit." Alexis ordered. "I cooked your daughter's favorite meal. You would know what that was if you hadn't been a bad wolf."

Malcolm's head lowered in a bow as he motioned toward the chair at the other end of the table.

"He doesn't have to take orders from you," Braelin snarled.

Things were escalating. I hated this but I knew Braelin and I didn't have any control over the situation. The normal part of me wanted to argue and resist but living as a werewolf the past several months and seeing Rikki remain calm under stressful moments had taught me a lot.

I tried to channel her and breathed in and out slowly.

"Braelin. Please."

Her eyes shifted to mine, sensing my urgency. Braelin glanced back at Alexis, then to our father who was now seated before taking a deep breath she had been holding.

"You do know my sister is happily mated to an Alpha who has no problem coming here to kick your ass and bring her home."

The fork Alexis had been holding flew out of her hand with accurate precision. Braelin stumbled back, taken by surprise. She struggled to inhale, letting out a guttural sound and I could feel Alexis's magic as she forced my sister to drop harshly to her knees.

My eyes widened as Braelin yanked the fork lodged in her neck. Blood gushed out of the three holes in her throat, and she flung it to the ground. Despite the pain, Braelin sat tall on her knees, eyes monstrous as she called to her wolf. But as if her flame had gone out, the gold in her eyes diminished. She fought but lost against the compulsion Alexis sent her way, hands dropping flat on the stone surface.

I moved swiftly, dropping down beside her and shouted to our father to grab anything that would help control the bleeding. I knew being a werewolf she wouldn't die, and the bleeding would stop soon but my instinct and fear made me fall into my paramedic habits.

"What the hell is wrong with you?" I shrieked and glanced up to find no remorse on Alexis's face.

Alexis lifted her empty glass from the table and sauntered over to us, kneeling beside Braelin.

When she reached for my sister, I pushed her arm away. Her eyes lifted, sapphire and black, decorated with a warning label that told me to back away.

"I will kill your sister!" It was all the threat she needed to force me not to stop her again.

This time Alexis's fingers curled around the back of Braelin's neck, squeezing tightly as if milking a cow. Braelin was unable to move from Alexis's firm grasp, blood dripping into the glass.

Tears fell from my eyes, and I looked up to see my father looking away. I could tell he was fighting his wolf not to react.

When her glass was filled to her satisfaction, Alexis stood and walked back to her seat.

Claws scratched against the stone surface of the floor as Braelin snarled, ready to shift. Rage and embarrassment brought Braelin's wolf to a breaking point, and she wanted to regain the dominance Alexis had taken so easily.

I lifted Braelin's chin, at eye level just as the holes in her throat began to close. An injury like that was not life threatening but seeing my sister in pain was horrific. I ran my fingers through her coiled hair. Taking a deep breath, I called out to my Omega. I couldn't let her shift or Alexis would have her killed.

Braelin's eyes looked past me toward Alexis, teeth grinding together, battling the yearning to shift.

"You think you're untouchable but you're far from it."

"Can I eat her?" Jaleel asked, leaning against the wall near the entryway. He nibbled on his bottom lip like a starving predator waiting for leftovers.

I held my hand up, "Please! Just give me a moment. I'll calm her down."

"I'm done playing nice. She's a—"

I covered Braelin's mouth before she could finish. My eyes simmered a dark gold, trapping my sister like a deer caught in headlights. Before she said something that would end this night with me in grief, I needed to take control of the situation. There was a lot about my abilities I'd yet to discover, and I had a feeling I was close to learning something new about me. "You want me to see him kill you?" I asked my sister in a low and raucous tone. Magic swirled around and through me like electricity, confident in what I needed to do. "You promised to trust me, and you are not keeping your word."

Braelin's forehead creased, finding my power unfamiliar.

I curled my magic around Braelin like a soft blanket and took away all the rage filled inside her like a hot air balloon. Leisurely, the stiffness in her shoulders subsided, expression softening and eyes drooping lazily.

The High Priestess, Mira, had told me that my Omega's abilities were created by black witch's. That without them, I wouldn't be what I was. She said magic lived within every supernatural and that it leaked out in diverse ways. What I first saw as a hindrance or obligation, I now channeled proudly as a gift.

"You should rest," I encouraged through my magic.

Braelin sighed. "I can't leave you."

Though she wanted to stay, all her energy was seeping out of her and into me.

I kissed her forehead. "I will be fine. She will never hurt me." I looked toward Alexis, who was sipping on my sister's blood. I maintained my own anger. My hold on my sister would snap if I allowed my emotions to get the better of me.

"Could our father take her somewhere decent to rest?" I asked.

Alexis took her time responding as she studied my father.

"Would you like that?" she asked him.

Malcolm looked at me, then Braelin before nodding. It hurt to see the same man my sister described as strong and untamable acting quite the opposite. I turned away, not able to face him.

In a quick gesture, Alexis waved her hand for them to leave.

"I am not leaving my sister," Braelin complained, sitting sluggishly on her knees.

"She'll be fine." Malcolm walked gingerly around the table. He knelt beside us, and our eyes locked in an instant. He could see my disappointment and I hated myself for judging him.

For better or worse, he was my father too and he deserved my respect. I tried to picture the man I first met when he saved me from falling off the cliff. That man seemed single-minded and forthright. I knew he was still in there and had to trust he was appearing weaker in front of Alexis for a reason.

I ran the tips of my fingers over Braelin's throat, making sure she was fully healed, and sighed when I saw nothing there. I kissed her cheek like a parent soothing her child. Anytime my Omega trickled out, it was like my role as baby sister or newly turned wolf was reversed. It was my job to soothe a wolf's anxiety and pain.

"You are an Omega," my father whispered, evidently unaware.

This time when I looked into his eyes, I didn't feel anything but deep gratitude for him being here.

I smiled. "Yeah. Not something I walk around sharing since half the werewolf community wants to kill or claim me. But I guess, vampire witches do too," I joked.

There was a slight crack in his blank expression as his eyes lit up.

"She'll be fine."

I nodded and stood, taking a step back to give them space. I watched as Malcolm encouraged Braelin to stand, not forcing her. Despite wanting to argue, Braelin glanced at me briefly and nodded her compliance to leave. A recent trick I'd learned was the ability to persuade by lessening someone's need to fight or resist.

"Finally," Alexis grumbled. "Thought that impudent sister of yours would never leave."

I turned to find Alexis still sitting in her chair, cozy and relaxed with my sister's blood in her glass. Defiantly, I walked toward her, snatching the glass from her hand, and slamming it on the floor, shattering it into tiny pieces. If Alexis wanted to, she could have moved her hand quickly enough to prevent me from taking the glass.

Instead, she stared down at the ground, finding my anger amusing. That only infuriated me more.

"You know. I'm trying to see the woman I once cared about, but all I see is the monster who has no soul. Who stalked me? Tricked me. Sent fucking ghouls after me. Killed innocent humans—"

Alexis swiftly stood and curled her fingers around my throat and squeezed. Her eyes were like the ones I remembered when I helped pull Amber's vampire, Benjamin, from her control. Black and sapphire. She pulled me close, our faces inches apart, and for a second, I thought she was going to try and compel me. It would be the only way for her to get me to do what she wanted.

When she noticed my guarded posture, all her anger vanished, and she shoved me away. Alexis turned, hunched over the table. She pressed both of her hands against the table, mumbling something before speaking louder.

"If you want a monster, I can show you what that looks like. I can bring your sister back in here and allow Jaleel to eat her like a fucking turkey!" she bellowed, her entire body shaking with rage. "And unmannered," she added.

I'd been swept by my own anger and triggered her with words she hated to hear. I shouldn't care what words hurt her, but I did. The Goddess help me, but I did. I still loved her. Not the same way I loved Rikki, but there was love.

"Again, I had no intention of killing any humans. I am deeply regretful of how I handled things. But I will not take fault in the idea of tricking you. Toyed with you, yes. But I never tricked you. You felt our connection whether you understood it or not. That is why I was easily able to access your mind when you slept. I am not perfect, but I am no monster. Especially when I know I can be, and I have been. Who doesn't go mad after living a very long life? Ask your Alpha about that."

Alexis's tone insinuated that she knew something about Rikki's past that I didn't. Rikki once shared with me about her time as a rogue and Tato being there to pull her out of that dark place. I knew there was a lot more to the story, but I never pushed. Now was not the time to worry about Rikki's past and I certainly wouldn't be discussing it with Alexis.

Several seconds passed with no words spoken. Alexis shifted, lifting a hand to her face and I felt the need to check on her. I knew she was right about what she'd said. She'd never tricked me. That had been confirmed after one of my dreams. I'd been pulled into an enthrall of sensing and feeling Alexis's touch but never mentally persuaded.

There was a lot to process, and I didn't want to blame her for my confused thoughts.

"Rachelle." I hesitated and decided to reach in, pressing my hand over her back.

Her head jerked and I witnessed a crimson tear slip from her eye, down her cheek. I stared, shocked and saddened. Her tear was blood. A mix of fear and anger flashed across her face before softening into a gentle smile. Something was deeply wrong with Alexis and the more time I spent with her, I could see she was unraveling. Some part of her emotions was severed, as if a light flickered in her mind and disoriented her at times.

I'd learned that vampires could shut off their humanity, but instinct told me there was more to her current situation. I sighed and cupped her cheek and at this moment, I could see her. Rachelle. The woman I adored and longed to marry once. The natural brown of her irises was back. The elegant glow of her brown skin and perfectly thick hair was as I remembered it.

"Why am I here?" I quietly whispered. There was more she wasn't sharing.

It was Rachelle's eyes that widened from my question. I could see the temptation to tell me, but she kept her mouth closed. Her eyes dipped toward my lips, and I mentally prayed for her not to kiss me. I didn't want to upset her again. But I also didn't want to feel those feelings I'd never completely gotten over. I couldn't. And I shouldn't want to.

"I can't tell you. Not yet," she mumbled as if trying to keep our conversation private.

"Why not?" I asked.

Her fingers combed through my messy braided hair. She took her time refamiliarizing herself with my hair and skin.

"Because...you are not ready."

Jaleel walked in and that snapped me out from Rachelle's proximity, taking a step back. He smirked when he saw my frantic behavior until he noticed Rachelle's icy glare. And there she was again. Alexis. The vampire, black witch.

"Forgive me," he whispered. "There is an affair that needs your attention."

Alexis nodded and turned to me. "I am sorry to cut this short. Please eat as much food as you like. And I suppose you shouldn't starve a hungry wolf so one of my servants will bring enough for your sister and father too."

"Where are you going?" I asked.

Alexis's smile was perfectly placed, never hinting that a tear had fallen from her eyes moments ago.

"Don't be greedy. We just shared an intimate moment." Without permission, Alexia kissed my cheek and left at a speed I wasn't used to before I had the chance to protest.

"Great," I complained, hands on my hips. I hated being left in the dark, especially if it involved me.

Chapter Three

Jaleel watched me from a distance, amused by my presence as usual. He gave me the same standoffish attitude Llyod used to give me. I had no doubt that Jaleel was loyal to Alexis, and I was the interloper that could put his master a risk.

"Having fun?" I sneered.

Jaleel moved off the wall and stood, straightening his jacket. He maintained an arrogant smirk.

"I take no pleasure in watching a confused girl." He turned and walked off before I could respond.

I gritted my teeth, following him at a distance. I wasn't going to explain myself to him, but his words still managed to cut deeply. I loved Rikki and would never betray her and yet Jaleel was right. I was conflicted. Not about my devotion to Rikki but my devotion to the past. I thought I'd let Rachelle go but it only took a few minutes for me to question myself when I woke up to the sight of her sitting over me. The woman who'd been taunting me was the same woman I'd cried over for countless nights. Our love was real, and I knew if Alexis hadn't left, we'd still be together now, however blind I would have been. Perhaps, she would have eventually shared the truth with me.

I halted, nearly bumping into Jaleel who'd stopped and turned to face me. Warily, I took a step back unsure of why he stopped. I suddenly felt claustrophobic in the hallway we'd been walking through. There were too many corridors and not enough open spaces, like walking in an endless maze. I shifted one leg back, ready to lunge if he attacked.

Jaleel hissed, fangs exposed and eyes turning pitch black. He stretched his arm toward the path we were walking.

"Continue this way and you will find your sister and father. Do not detour or defy my master or your sister will pay the price."

I blinked as Jaleel moved with inhuman speed past me and I jolted backward, pressed against the wall. I looked toward the direction we'd come from, suspecting there was trouble. I hesitated, not sure whether to continue toward my sister or investigate what was transpiring. I knew Jaleel was going to Alexis by the look in his eyes.

I sighed, knowing I needed to be smart, and headed to my sister. The long hall never changed paths until I reached a living space where a fireplace was lit, warming the room.

"Over here," Malcolm called out.

I looked to my right, finding Malcolm sitting over Braelin asleep on a couch. I moved quickly to my sister's side, Malcolm taking a step back. Kneeling beside Braelin, I ran the tips of my fingers along the side of her face. She looked peaceful despite the pain she had suffered at the hands of Alexis.

I frowned and shut my eyes, guilt settling inside my chest. Alexis had done this to her and yet I still struggled to hate her. I still saw Rachelle through Alexis's dark eyes.

"This is not your fault." Malcolm took a seat on the couch alongside Braelin and hunched over to the coffee table where a platter of food resided, food we had brought from the dining hall before things went to hell.

Brows furrowed, I twisted my head and watched him before speaking.

"Why did Alexis say you placed yourself in the position to be enslaved to her?"

Malcolm's shoulders straightened, brows creasing in dismay, with every intention of avoiding my question.

"It doesn't—"

"If you say it doesn't matter, I'm calling bullshit," I cut him off, not in the mood to hear him dismiss my question or make up some excuse. He wanted the conversation to be dropped but if I was going to trust him, it meant he needed to tell us the truth. Braelin might have a blind spot to our father, but I didn't know him and found his absence suspicious.

"Alexis will twist words around and deceive you if you let her. Don't fall for it. She is as evil as it gets." Malcolm said, and shut his eyes, fingers pressing into the bridge of his nose.

It was easy for me to pounce on him with more questions, but Malcolm was seconds away from emotionally shutting down. I sucked in a breath, rethinking my approach. He was the only ally we had and putting us at odds wouldn't help our circumstances.

Carefully, I repositioned Braelin's sleeping body, sliding back onto the couch, and laying her head over my lap. Braelin wasn't a heavy sleeper, but the blood loss and my magic had drained her more than I expected. I suspected she hadn't slept since we arrived.

"I can't believe I have a daughter who is an Omega," Malcolm blurted out, a smile stretched across his face.

I ran my fingers through the edges of Braelin's hair and sighed.

"Not the reaction I expected."

"Why wouldn't I be happy about that?" he questioned.

"Because it means I'm in constant danger," I clarified. "Not something I would think a parent would want for their child, that kind of hardship."

Malcolm frowned. "That's a human's perspective. Always afraid of a good thing." His words were honest. He leaned forward, elbows pressed into his knees as he watched me sooth Braelin. "You are a gift, more than you know. That comes with risk but so does your birthright."

It was my turn to frown. "What do you mean?"

"Being an Adisa carries a lot of weight. Why do you think you're here?" Malcolm asked.

I shrugged. Clearly, he knew more than he was saying.

"To convince me to donate my blood for her survival."

Malcolm snorted. "She's a black witch. You really think she didn't find a way around the spell cast on her?"

I didn't know Alexis, but I knew Rachelle. She could be very driven and unrelenting when she needed something. Nothing could stop her from figuring out a solution.

"Then why am I here?"

Malcolm shook his head. "I can't answer that."

"You mean you won't," I argued.

He nodded. "I won't and I can't because Alexis compelled me not to, but you also aren't ready to know everything yet."

I was already tired of hearing that but there was no point in arguing. If he was compelled, it didn't matter what I said, he wouldn't tell me. I thought about my mom and then the woman I'd never get to meet and grimaced. What was special about my birth mother? And what did that mean for me? Recently, I'd been curious about my past and here was the opportunity to ask Malcolm questions.

I peeked down at Braelin and rested my arm across her body.

"Who was Sonia Adisa?" I nibbled on my bottom lip anxiously, and I knew depending on what he said next my walls might come up.

Malcolm's demeanor shifted, his shoulders stiffening. Several long heartbeats later, Malcolm readjusted and exhaled.

"You remind me of her."

I tried not to doubt his words but part of me wondered if he said that to make me feel closer to a mother I would never meet. He didn't know me, something I hoped would change in time. I continued to listen, afraid if I spoke, he'd change his mind about sharing.

"Stubborn, honest, and very expressive." He chuckled, clearly reliving a memory. "Very empathetic to others." He quickly wiped the tear huddled at the corner of his eye and cleared his throat. "When I met her…I was already indebted to Alexis."

Was he about to tell me the real reason he'd become enslaved to Alexis? I sat quietly, trying not to show my eagerness. I wasn't a fan of being left in the dark and it meant more than he knew to hear his story.

"Braelin doesn't know this." He glanced at my sister, making sure she wasn't awake before he continued. "After we'd been turned, it wasn't easy having to worry about my temper, let alone a teenager. Money was always tight, and we were on the verge of being homeless. And after I gave your sister—" Malcolm took a deep breath, staring up at the ceiling to control his emotions. “Your mother, I suppose you’d call her. Losing Breanne was a devastating time for both of us. So, I thought if I kept busy, I could forget about our loss. We were new werewolves and raising a toddler was dangerous for her.”

“I understand.” I couldn’t imagine the position he and Braelin had been put in.

“I was hired as a contractor and at the time I didn’t know who’d I’d been employed by. I accepted through a third party.” Malcolm’s brows slanted inward, regret spreading across his face.

“What do you mean, you were hired as a contractor?” I asked.

His eyes widened, realizing he’d probably shared more than he intended. It was too late for him to take his words back.

“You can say I was whatever was needed to get paid. Bounty hunter. A brute force. And sometimes, on rare occasions, an assassin.”

I tried not to let my shock show.

“I’d served in the military and was quite capable,” he explained. “Not my proudest moments but I never killed the innocent.” Malcolm ran his fingers through his cropped coiled hair, working hard to get through the story. “I was asked to act as a private investigator. My unknown client needed me to find someone and watch them. That someone was Sonia.”

I nodded. His story was far more revealing than I expected.

“Long story short, I ended up doing more than watching her from a distance. She was like a ray of light from the sun and drew me in. I fell in love with her.”

"Did she know?" I asked. His answer mattered to me. He'd potentially put her in harm's way and the least he could have done was to be honest as to why they'd met.

He nodded. "Eventually, I told her the truth. It was the day she told me she was pregnant with you."

Uncomfortable, I shifted my gaze away. Was I ready to hear the rest of this? I wondered if the truth would change me, but it was too late to back down now. If I couldn't handle this, I wouldn't be able to handle the secrets he or Alexis hadn't shared yet.

"My whole world changed that day. I told her the truth and expected her to run but she did the opposite," Malcolm stated, a smile shining through his eyes. "She told me she already knew and forgave me. My client hadn't announced herself or requested anything for months and I thought maybe she'd changed her mind until I was requested to meet." He ran the palms of his hands over his pants and grimaced.

"It was Alexis. She told me that I needed to bring Sonia to her, and I said no." Malcolm took a moment to catch his breath, becoming overwhelmed. "She said if I refused it would be considered a breach of contract. Let's just say, I did the only thing I could think of. I went back to Sonia, told her the truth, and we ran."

"And left Braelin alone?" I questioned, a newfound sadness swelling in my chest. Braelin had told me what she knew but from her perspective, he'd found a new family and left her. I wanted to be angry at Malcolm but listened, open to hearing his side.

"If Braelin had come with us, she would be dead or enslaved to Alexis too," Malcolm spoke adamantly.

I could see that and understood why he left her behind.

"She eventually knew you'd gotten into trouble, and it had to do with Sonia, but your leaving came across as abandonment. You have no idea what she's been through."

"I thought of her every day," Malcolm admitted. "And when you were born, it was the one time I ever witnessed such emotional torture and fear in your mothers' eyes when we had to give you away. I thought…the least I could do was keep you with family. I always knew where my daughter Breanne was and met her husband several years prior. I'd shared the truth with him and told him, one day I might need him, and he never wavered."

Hearing about the man who raised me, tears fell from my eyes. I knew Darnell had known for years what I was, and I had wondered if my dad had known too. This answered my question. He more than knew and had played a crucial part in keeping me alive. It made me love him even more.

I wasn't ready to hear of my birth mother's death, but I was curious about something else.

"So, Alexis had enslaved you because you'd broken a contract? And going after Sonia was all for her blood?"

Malcolm hesitated and this was where I knew he'd hold back information.

"I am indebted to her due to my break in contract, yes."

My brows furrowed, expecting to hear more.

"Bonnie. It was little to do with your blood and her will to survive and more to do with who your mother was." Malcolm spoke carefully, making sure not to say too much.

"And who was she?" I pressed.

"The same thing you are." He spoke vaguely.

I sighed mentally, knowing he was done sharing. I needed to process what he'd said. I wondered how he and my birth mother had managed to hide for months and keep me hidden years after. Another question came to mind, but I didn't bother asking him. He wouldn't tell me. I was a born werewolf, but it had taken a near death experience to awaken my wolf when Cain, a werewolf who had his own agenda, attacked me in hopes to claim me. Braelin had been nothing more than a stranger to me at the time, searching for me after years of pretending I didn't exist. I wondered what secrets I'd eventually uncover because I wasn't going to leave this cave until I knew everything.

Chapter Four

We sat in silence for several long minutes before someone approached. It wasn't Alexis or Jaleel, not even the very self-aware ghoul, Arlana. A boy, about ten, with cloudy grey eyes and murky brown hair stepped into view. He wore a bothered expression as if he'd been summoned here in the middle of a videogaming session. He was not human, and I rolled my eyes knowing exactly what he was.

The changeling eyes scrutinized me first before speaking.

"It seems your mate has been causing quite an amount of trouble."

I leaped off the couch, startling Braelin awake.

"Rikki. Where is she?"

"Close enough." The changeling trapped in a boy's body said. "Seems your mate has better connections than our master thought," he spoke directly to Malcolm. "Made a deal with a changeling I know."

Instantly, I knew who he was referring to.

"Maerel, that crazy little girl."

The boy's eyes rolled in what looked like disdain. Clearly, he recognized her name. I didn't care. Rikki was near and that's all that mattered.

"You are being summoned," he said.

I moved toward the boy without a second thought.

"Wait," Braelin snarled.

"You are to stay put." The boy looked at Malcolm. "If she leaves, she will have signed your death sentence," he said coldly. It was an eerie feeling, witnessing the grueling scowl the boy gave my father.

This was my chance to protect Braelin even though she wouldn't see it that way.

"I request her presence at my side," I demanded. It was awkward trying to obtain permission from someone long lived in a little boy's body. He looked innocent enough to pass as a normal child, riding his bike and playing hide and seek with other kids. But instead, I was met with a changeling that made me want to be cautious around every adorable child I saw from here on out.

"You are not permitted to make such a decision," the changeling stated. His expression pinched in annoyance at my statement.

"I have the free will to leave anytime, correct?" By his sour expression, I knew I'd used the right words.

It had become clear that Alexis needed my corporation, unable to keep me otherwise. I watched him carefully like an opponent in a chess match and waited for his response.

"I won't get in trouble for you," he complained.

"I'll make sure she knows you had no choice," I promised.

His eyes washed over Braelin before walking off.

Braelin hesitated between our father and me.

Malcolm smiled. "I'll be fine. I've lived this long."

She nodded and moved to the door.

It took several minutes and a lot of passages until we reached what resembled a long hall. Bright light shone through a distant opening, and I suspected we were at the main entrance of the cave. I stood off to the side of the hall and took in the cavernous space.

A cardinal rug stretched from the throne where Alexis stood, raised a few steps above the intricate grandeur. The stone walls were smooth and illuminated by lusters that showcased centuries old paintings of creatures I'd never learned in my supernatural lessons. Alexis hovered in front of the dark magnificent granite throne seat covered in baroque patterns. The bulky cushions were dark maroon, also adorned by embroidery.

Alexis hadn't changed from the dress she'd worn at the short-lived dinner. Her eyes seeped onto me and softened before noticing my sister beside me.

Before she could scold the boy, I took the lead.

"I persisted and made it clear I wouldn't come without her."

There was a long pause before she decided her next words.

"Come and sit beside me."

I noticed a second chair, smaller than hers and frowned. She wanted to make us look unified and I wouldn't do that.

The disappointment in her eyes was replaced with a stoic demeanor.

I heard footsteps approach and knew who it was before I could see her. That rosemary and oak scent perfumed my nose and I inhaled, warmth settling inside me.

I ignored Jaleel, watching as Rikki, Amber, Shiloh, and Maerel came into view. I lurched with excitement, moving to rush into Rikki's long arms when I was halted by an unseen force. Her eyes, a stormy gray, never left mine. Her relief at seeing me was evident in the way her toned shoulders loosened enough for me to see her breathe. Alexis's magic kept me from running to Rikki and I didn't try to move again, knowing that it would only enrage Alexis and she would take it out on Braelin later.

Rikki stiffened, sensing my distress, and snarled. "Let her go!"

It was like being wrapped in a straitjacket from head to toe. As much as I wanted to fight, I was unable to move.

Alexis's hand was stretched out in my direction, controlling my body. I'd yet to witness her powers personally and now knew how it felt to be powerless. I hated it.

"I swear, if you don't let me go, Rachelle!" I screamed out, calling her by the name I'd once said as her lover.

"Rachelle?" Rikki questioned, stunned. By the bizarre glare in Rikki's eyes, she recognized Rachelle's name. I wondered how Rikki didn't look surprised by who Rachelle was since I'd never mentioned her name.

Alexis gradually lowered her arm and her hold on me slowly diminished. She clapped her hands together as if dusting dirt from her hands before taking a seat.

"I won't ask you again!"

She was talking to me. The last thing she wanted me to do was embarrass her in front of everyone by simply denying her.

I took a moment to gather my thoughts, peering at my mate. Rikki was beautiful and fierce. Ready to take on the whole world.

Shiloh nodded, reminding me not to neglect Alexis's request. He was great at seeing both sides, Alexis's and Rikki's, and that made him a great leader for Oregon.

I moved toward Alexis and sighed, sitting beside her. Jaleel moved to his master and sat on the opposite end. Now her throne was complete.

I watched the smug expression curl Alexis's full lips. Alexis planted the palms of her hands over the black armrest of her seat, crossing her legs.

Rikki's eyes danced from Alexis to me, and I was thankful to find her smiling and not angry. She knew I wished to be in her arms right now and that gave me relief. It meant a lot to know she trusted me.

"Rachelle," Rikki said again, this time more slowly. She snorted and looked at her brother and then Amber, who didn't seem to understand what was happening. Rikki looked at me.

"You know…when you told me about her and how she magically vanished…instinct told me that she was probably more than you knew. After all, you were always a werewolf underneath that human façade. And I'm sure she knows a lot more about your lineage."

When Rikki had taken me on a weekend trip to Portland, I'd shared my past and how broken I was to lose Rachelle. I hadn't planned to share my memories of Rachelle that night, but I was thankful I did now.

"How'd you know her name? I don't remember mentioning that part," I asked.

"Your mother told me. She thinks you needed a break and left for a couple days. Had to come up with something."

I tried not to flinch. I wanted to say that I would never leave Rikki's side however hard it got but here I was now, sitting beside another woman. I did it to keep everyone safe until a better plan could form but I'd left. I thought about me leaving willingly now and realized Rikki's explanation for my mom wasn't too far off from the truth.

Rikki continued. "She thought I should know how hard you took losing the woman you were supposed to spend the rest of your life with and how vulnerable you were being falling in love with me." Rikki had no problem sharing this openly in front of Alexis and the others.

I nodded and told myself to give my mom a big hug when I saw her again, for always watching over me even when I wouldn't allow her to.

"You both are losing me," Amber scowled in frustration. "I thought this vampire witch bitch's name was Alexis." Amber shifted a reviled glance at Alexis and gave a half attempt at bowing. "My apologies. Vampire Sire, right?" she sneered.

"Short story," Shiloh said, nonchalantly. "Alexis is also known as Rachelle, who happens to be Bonnie's old lover."

It was Maerel's turn to give input. "You are full of surprises, Ms. Collins," she said in her innocent child voice.

Jokingly, I asked, "Won't your mother be worried if you don't get home by bedtime?"

Maerel's smile reached all the way to her eyes.

"I finally ate her and now I'm in search of a new mommy. Care to be mine?"

I shuddered from revulsion and looked away. I'd known there was a dark side to Maerel but only prayed she was joking. The smile on her face increased and I knew what that look meant. She'd helped Rikki find this place through her link with the boy changeling.

I'd now owe her two favors. If I counted the favors owed, it would be two for Maerel and one for the High Priestess, Mira.

"Enough," Alexis spoke with a sharp tongue. "I've entertained you all long enough. The only reason I have allowed you access is because of my own curiosity about the Alpha who claims to be mated to the woman I adore."

There was a possessiveness in her tone I didn't care for, but I kept my mouth shut. No sense in pissing her off more.

"If you care for her, then allow her to leave," Rikki said.

Alexis shifted a glance my way. "Have I treated you ill in any way?"

She wanted me to answer, and I knew if I didn't there would be a consequence. Even though she'd done and said a few things, they'd been more directed at my sister. I glanced past Alexis, where Braelin stood quiet and unmoving.

"No," I muttered.

"See!" Alexis stretched her hands out. "Bonnie is safe with me."

"She'll be safer with her pack and at my side," Rikki challenged.

Alexis coughed out a laugh, finding Rikki's remark amusing.

"I doubt that." Alexis reached out and gently ran the back of her finger down my cheek. I shuddered, mentally pleading for her to stop. She was letting out a lot of pheromones, suffocating me in her lust for me. It made my body respond without my consent and I frowned.

It also made Rikki react with an impulse to put Alexis in her place.

"Don't touch her!" she warned. I felt the heat radiating out of Rikki, and I knew if she didn't calm down, she'd shift and try to kill Alexis.

Jaleel would protect Alexis, giving Rikki no chance at reaching me before Alexis grabbed and fled with me wrapped in her arms. I watched as the reptilian vympyrus shifted in his seat, mentally pleading for Rikki to attack. He was in his true form today, tongue slithering out in anticipation.

Alexis looked at me. "You are free to leave at any time," she said, waving her arm toward Rikki in invitation.

I swallowed what felt like my entire trachea, knowing it wasn't as easy as she made it sound. There was a reason I'd willingly come. Alexis wouldn't stop being a threat to the ones I loved. She wasn't going to just allow me to leave and say, *at least I tried.*

"I choose to stay by your side." I looked up at Rikki hoping she understood. I hated how that sounded coming out of my mouth. Alexis was happy, but I wasn't, and I would make sure she knew that when this was over.

There was a slight look of hurt in Rikki's eyes, but she let out a long breath and nodded. She understood and my heart pounded, relief setting in.

"See." Alexis beamed, not holding back her arrogance. "She's very content." Alexis slid to the edge of her seat, body slanted, craning her neck with inquisitiveness. "Now that you see she is well taken care of, you will have this one opportunity to leave unharmed. Come again, and I'll slaughter all of you."

"You surely don't sound like the loving woman Bonnie described." Rikki dismissed Alexis and pushed with words that I knew were triggers. "What darkness possessed you or have you always had immorality?"

There was a stillness in Alexis's posture like a snake right before it sprang for a bite. Rikki's words hit home, and I wondered if she was hinting at something.

My heart pounded in my ears, and I took the chance given before Alexis made a choice I would never want to see. I reached across the chair and touched her arm, calling out my Omega to assist me. Alexis resisted my wolf's magic but whispering her name was all it took to lure her to my magic like a trap.

"Rachelle. Please don't do anything rash."

For a fleeting moment there was insecurity slipping out from Alexis's exterior. I watched a twitch at the corner of her eye, her fangs lengthening. She was fighting something inside. It was the second time I noticed something off about Alexis and it made me feel regret. I'd dismissed her words when she said she had no choice in leaving me. Perhaps she didn't have a choice but what did that mean?

"I have no intention of leaving you. Not until I see the woman I once loved in those brown eyes of yours." I whispered too low for anyone else to hear. I wasn't naïve. I had no real choice in the matter, but I wouldn't let my time here go to waste. I believed the woman I once loved was real and authentic and whoever I was sitting beside now was something dark that had taken over. Something had happened to her for her to leave me, and I needed to know what that was.

Alexis was silent long enough to assure me she had been listening. She kept absolute silence, her expression crumbling from whatever truth she was keeping.

I breathed in relief and moved my hand away. All eyes were on me, and I lifted my head up, not cowering from their confused glares.

"Now that you have come, uninvited, and have seen she is well taken care of there is no reason for you to stay." Alexis wasn't asking.

Shiloh stood, arms crossed over his chest, bored and annoyed. When he noticed me looking, he bowed his head in understanding. His hair had been cut recently, cropped with an undercut. I missed the ponytail. His native features stood out more, squared chin covered with a light beard forming.

"It is apparent we all want what's best for Bonnie," he said.

Rikki's neck craned, shifting an inimical glance at her brother.

He stretched his arms out, gesturing for peace.

"Hear me out." His brow arched, giving Rikki a few seconds to listen. "As you can see, Bonnie is fine. And as much as we aren't pleased by the remarkable vampire witch's actions, she has no intention of causing her harm. From what I can see, she's protecting her." He smiled toward Alexis, knowing he was right. "The question is from whom? Something happened, forcing you to act. My guess, you would have never revealed yourself to Bonnie if her life wasn't in danger."

I frowned and pivoted my gaze Alexis's way. She gave no acknowledgement of his statement, an expression unreadable. Was Shiloh right?

"No offense." Amber gestured from me to Rikki before bringing her attention to Alexis, her stance fierce and ready for anything. "I am here to collect my vampire. I don't know what he's done but Portland is my city."

Alexis snorted. "Portland was never yours. I allowed you to come in, that is all."

Amber took a step, triggering Jaleel to stand.

The tension between Amber and Alexis was boiling and I knew all it would take was a simple gesture for Jaleel to launch himself at the Sire of Portland. I didn't doubt Amber's strength, but Jaleel wasn't going to be easy to defeat.

"You are far from being power hungry," I jumped in, wanting to diffuse the situation. "If you were, you would have done far more."

Alexis pursed her lips before waving her hand for Jaleel to sit.

"Your vampire, Benjamin. That is who you are referring to?" She asked coyly.

For a long second, Amber struggled to gather her words without acting out. "Yes!" she said through gritted teeth.

"He made a very greedy mistake," Alexis accused.

"Then you should have come to me." Amber wasn't in the mood for a long-drawn-out conversation. She was usually calm and playful but when one of her own was taken, there was no mistaking her deadly instinct.

Alexis chuckled. "I'll remember that for next time."

"What did he do?" Amber asked. She noticed Alexis's surprised reaction and clarified. "From one vampire sire to the next, I do not want him or any of my vampires making the same mistake." The conversation morphed into vampire politics from what I could understand.

All while they were exchanging words, I'd kept my eyes on Rikki who hadn't looked away from me yet. She mouthed *I love you* and I did the same. I missed her.

"The two humans I'd sent Jaleel to lure toward Bonnie at the dance club." At Alexis's mention of the two women Rikki and I had met at the dance club, my attention was back on her.

After one of the women had introduced themselves, we'd briefly sat with them at the table before going onto the dance floor. The last time I saw both was when one woman died on the dance floor while the other was found unconscious a few blocks away in a neighborhood. Amber's vampire, Benjamin, had been there, sick from drinking the woman's blood. But it had been more complicated than expected. Benjamin had been bitten by Jaleel, ultimately being pulled under Alexis's control through blood magic.

"She was my human servant and he'd attacked her," Alexis explained.

I frowned. "Human what…?" I asked, perplexed.

"I assure you, she was very willing to serve me in exchange that I one day turned her. I'm sure Amber has her share of human servants. You think she roams around the city turning humans? No! We groom them," Alexis explained.

The entire time I'd thought the two women were unwilling participants. My view of her shifted a little more. Maybe she wasn't as cruel as she pretended to be.

"In fact," Alexis sang out.

Footsteps approached from where Braelin and I had come from, and my eyes widened when both the women I'd thought were dead stood before us. It was Theresa and Sue, very much…wait. Not alive but undead. Behind them, Benjamin walked into view, head down with embarrassment.

He noticed Amber and walked toward her as she quickly moved to his side and guided him back beside Rikki and Shiloh.

I stood from shock and confusion. "I thought—"

"I know what you thought. They died, yes. But my blood was already coursing through their veins." Alexis moved with inhuman speed to her two new progenies and gave them each a kiss over their pale cheeks.

Sue smiled at her Sire's comfort before giving me an apologetic nod.

"It was our last test of loyalty before we were allowed to turn. A show of faith, dying for her."

I didn't know what to say but one thing was on my mind. How many supernaturals loyal to Alexis were in this cave?

"See. Even he's unharmed," Alexis stated.

Amber nodded. "He will atone for his actions through a strict punishment. My apologies for him attacking one of yours," she said, diplomatically.

Now that things were settled between them it was back to my mate and Alexis's standoff.

Rikki decided to speak first. "I have no intention of leaving my mate behind."

There was a darkness that suddenly swarmed around Alexis's posture, and I knew she wasn't going to give me up. She certainly wasn't a fan of being told what to do.

"Can I speak to my mate alone?" I asked.

Alexis first instinct was to say no but she hesitated. For a split second I thought she'd approve, holding my breath.

"No, but you are free to approach her."

That was better than nothing. I stood and walked across the hall until I was within reach of my mate. Tears left my eyes the moment Rikki pulled me into a tight embrace. I sighed, sinking into her, happy to feel her body pressed against mine.

Our lips eventually met as I breathed in her scent like I always did. She was warm and comforting. I wrapped my arms around her waist, our lips pulling away a few seconds later.

"I've missed you."

"Come back with me," Rikki whispered. She knew I had to stay but the wolf in her couldn't let go. I could see Rikki's wolf pacing. Heard the growling low in her chest.

It hurt to see Rikki so conflicted with the need to tear me from Alexis and the desire to respect my decision.

"Trust me, I want to. But things between Alexis…" I paused, needing to be completely honest with her. "Things between Rachelle and I are unfinished. And I don't want to come back confused and regretful of not finally putting the past behind me." I sighed, another tear sliding down my cheek. Rikki's lie about me leaving was beginning to sound more accurate. "Besides, she'd only create havoc for us again and she knows things that I need to know."

"I am in love with you. And I will always choose you," I continued. "And as much as it is scary to admit, some part of me still loves Rachelle and I must face her to let it go. And I owe it to our memory to do that and help her find her way back because the woman on that throne isn't all she is."

Rikki understood what I was saying, and I knew it hurt her to hear my truth. I couldn't go back home with another woman on my mind. It was unfair and selfish. I thought Rachelle was my past and would stay there but I was wrong.

"I hate this, but I will support you. Not that I agree. You can learn to let her go while at home with me. But I will always support you because I know you'll be home soon." Rikki kissed me again with more passion than I'd felt in all the months we'd been together. When our lips parted I felt myself gasping for air. Her stoic expression was back and directed at Alexis.

"I think we can come to some arrangement."

Alexis didn't say anything right away. Her gaze lingered on me, jealous from my encounter with Rikki.

I walked back to Alexis and took a seat, feeling apprehensive and indecisive but my decision had already been made. I told myself I needed to stay for closure but in the back of my mind, maybe it was for more than that. There were answers I needed, and I couldn't leave here without Malcolm and without knowing the secret Alexis was keeping from me.

"What do you have in mind?" Alexis asked.

"You point me in the direction of who you're so eager to protect my mate from and perhaps this can be resolved much faster," Rikki said.

Alexis shook her head. "I already have my—"

"Isn't it better for everyone to work together on this?" I interjected.

Alexis's expression soured. "I know I have let you speak but please don't cut me off," she muttered.

I clamped my mouth shut, embarrassed and not wanting Rikki to argue in my defense.

"When the time comes, I am willing to accept your assistance. But perhaps, you can be of use to me."

"How so?" Rikki asked, annoyed.

"I've been sealed to this cave, unable to leave. Find the witch responsible and convince her to release my hold. I've been courteous not to slaughter her entire coven for this long, but my patience is dissolving," Alexis said.

"Who's the witch?" Rikki asked.

"The same one who helped guide you here," she sneered.

Mira, the High Priestess of the black witch coven. I'd faced the High Priestess and she'd said nothing of being responsible for binding Alexis to the cave, implying it was long before her time. But perhaps she was far older than she looked. Everyone had their secrets and parts to play.

Rikki was smart and the last thing we needed was a war with a bunch of witches if she took on the request.

Chin raised, Rikki nodded once. “I will be back.”

Alexis frowned, considering, and nodded. “Fair enough. Now go or I might change my mind.”

“Take Braelin with you,” I shouted.

Braelin moved alongside the throne and took a step up the platform but was halted by Alexis’s magic blocking her like a barricade. The urge to punch through Alexis’s magic like breaking through a piñata braced Braelin’s shoulders and taut arms. She was furious at me.

“I said that I would stay by your side, and I meant that.”

I nodded. “I know. And I love you for it. But I also love you enough to need to see you breathing at the end of this.” Truth was, she was a liability staying here. I’d always worry about how I acted and spoke at the risk of Alexis or someone else using my sister as a punching bag or vein to open, in order to teach me a lesson. I wouldn’t be able to handle losing her over me or her own dominant personality. “You will help me more staying by Rikki’s side.” Mentally, leaning on our sisterly bond, I pleaded for her to listen.

Braelin directed her attention toward Alexis, tempted to say something, but kept her mouth shut and I was thankful. With nervous apprehension, Braelin walked toward Rikki accepting my request.

“Tell—"

“I know,” I said before she could finish. She feared never seeing our father again, but I refused to let him die after just meeting him. “And I will.”

Alexis had nothing more to say and Jaleel stood, taking the lead to guide them out.

"I'll be back," Rikki told me.

I smiled. "I know you will." It was hard being so far from her. Part of me wanted to change my mind and run into her arms. Leave Alexis to her own demise and believe that I'd forget her one day. But that would be unrealistic. I was there and Alexis was very much real and not someone to discard.

"Please be safe," I called out just as Rikki rounded the corner out of view.

Alexis continued to sit, fingers grazing her lips in deep thought. I gave her space to speak first, in need of my own personal time to process what just occurred.

Theresa and Sue waited for Alexis's permission to leave, standing side by side in formation.

When Alexis finally lifted her head, she nodded toward the two woman I thought were victims and they left with unrecognizable speed.

Alone, I waited for Alexis to speak first.

"We've always made a great team." Her voice was barely audible.

There was a time I would have had Alexis's back without question but for obvious reasons, things had changed.

"I want to trust you," I said.

"Then trust me and know I have nothing but pure intentions for you." Alexis was angry and I'd been the cause. "And don't mock our love."

"Mock?" I repeated bewildered.

"Flaunting yourself, in front of me. In front of my progenies," she stifled out. Her body shook and I didn't realize until now how much she'd worked to control her temper.

I wanted to be gentle with my words but there was no way around telling the truth without upsetting her. "Rikki is my mate. Was I supposed to pretend she was a stranger?"

"No, but you didn't need to let her touch or kiss you," Alexis sneered. "You were supposed to be my—"

"And you left me!" I roared, suddenly overwhelmed. I'd been trying to manage my hurt, but she wasn't helping. I stood, both my wolf and I pacing. "You left me. I fell apart. Was lost without you for over a year. Even after, I couldn't allow anyone else in, always hoping you'd pop back up."

"But then you met that Alpha," she hissed, begrudgingly.

"Yes!" I echoed, my chest heaving in and out. "Even then, without understanding until now, I was hesitant of being with her. Not just because I'd been thrown into a new world but because I was scared. Scared of falling in love only for them to disappear."

Alexis's face hardened.

"I. Had. No. Choice," she sneered, low and slow, eyes averting from mine.

"Right," I blew out. "Let me guess. You were cast here to be locked away for eternity," I said, dryly.

"No!" she argued.

"Then what? Did Mira find out you were cozied with an Adisa and feared you'd eventually devour and drain me of my blood?" I challenged. It was the first time I referred to myself as an Adisa. The name was unfamiliar to me and carried a lot of weight.

"I told you, I drink synthetic blood."

"How?" I questioned.

Alexis frowned.

"No, tell me. How, Rachelle?" Tears swelled in my eyes. "By killing my mother?" I stood still, waiting for the words I feared to hear.

Alexis's grim look told me all I needed to know.

In a fit of rage, I lashed out at her, fingers partially shifting into claws as I raked them across her face. Blood dripped from deep gashes stretched from below her right eye, nose, and upper lip, all the way across to her ear. I swung my arm again and Alexis didn't bother blocking me, taking the blow, this time down her neck to her collarbone. Blood oozed down her perfect dress, and I cried.

I could hear fast movement, expecting Jaleel or one of her other servants to grab me but no one came. It was hard to see with all the tears.

"How could you do that to me? Come into my life knowing what you did to my mother?"

"I'm sorry," Alexis whispered.

I tried wiping away the tears, but they kept coming. I felt hands brush my arm and I flinched, moving away.

"Are you going to kill me too and you're just acting like you loved me?" I said in malice. I knew I was being harsh, but I didn't care. As if my words weren't enough, I called to my wolf, and felt bones pop in my jaw as I partially shifted and sank my teeth into my forearm, drawing blood. Running my tongue along my teeth, only a couple had enlarged, causing the most damage to my skin.

"Here, make yourself right at home!" I said, offering my arm.

Blood dripped to the ground, and I looked up at Alexis, her attention not on my arm but past me. "Leave. Now!" she hissed.

Whatever presence that had been behind me was gone. I hadn't been paying attention to who was around.

Alexis leaned over, tearing a piece of her dress off and moved quickly, wrapping my arm.

"Not smart of you to open yourself up to a cave filled with vampires and ghouls," Alexis grumbled.

"Well, I'm not feeling very rational right now." I was far from rational. Angry, bitter, depressed.

Alexis cupped my chin, and I didn't move. "Your father will paint me as a monster who slaughtered his wife. But I am telling you, that is far from the truth."

"So, you didn't kill her?" I asked.

"I may as well have," she whispered.

Warily, I stared more confused than ever.

"What does that mean? Did you…or did you not kill my mother?"

"I've said more than enough." Alexis took a step back. "I will guide you to the room where you will be staying."

"Don't bother. At this point I'd prefer Jaleel over you." I crossed my arm and turned away.

Alexis only glared at me before nodding. "Fine. Have it your way," and left me standing alone.

Chapter Five

After being escorted back into the room, I fell asleep before I could pull the covers over me. Throughout the night, dreams came and went with no memory, keeping me on edge. But, somewhere in my dream state I knew it was the woman of my past stirring me in ways I'd rather not recollect.

Soft fingers grazed my hand before lightly brushing up my exposed arm. I thought of Rikki in my partially roused state and missed her body pressed against mine and the way she made me feel safe and loved. The way she opened herself up and let her vulnerable side show. Our intimacy not merely about sex but how we spoke to each other.

I let out a soft exhale when someone's fingers brushed my neck. I shuddered and air passed through my lips, wishing this were real and not a dream.

But soft lips caressed my neck, and I knew I wasn't dreaming.

I jolted awake reminding myself I wasn't home. Pressed close to my side, Alexis's eyes were a hollow black and sapphire. I was about to speak but instinct told me to stay silent. Something wasn't right, judging by the emptiness in her eyes.

The door opened and I slowly twisted my head, Jaleel coming to view. It was the first time I was thankful to see him. He didn't come closer, lingering by the door with concern for his master. Did he not realize I was the one in danger? Perhaps, he had an issue with perception.

"Play along. Don't exhibit fear and you will live for another day."

Was he serious? I was on the verge of screaming and he wanted me to play dead. I thought of the advice I heard growing up if confronted with a grizzly. To play dead. I never could believe that was the best choice. Or maybe it was that I didn't want to find out. But here I was now.

I wanted to know what was wrong with her but not from this angle.

"She hasn't fed," he whispered.

I tried not to look into her eyes, feeling one of her hands snaked across my waist, possessively.

"Why?" I whispered.

"Punishment," he stated.

Why was she punishing herself? I tried to consider but was too eerily aware of a dangerous vampire, stretched across and hunched over me.

"Leave us," Alexis muttered in a melodic tone.

Jaleel didn't hesitate and closed the door quietly.

"Alexis…" I whispered.

"Please don't call me that. You once loved Rachelle."

There was a longing to be loved again and I found myself brushing my hand along her cheek. I shut my eyes and licked my dry lips, terrified if I wasn't careful, she'd rip into my throat. Alexis watched the pulse vigorously bouncing along the curve of my neck, dancing for her to taste.

Pheromones leaked onto my skin like water. The sudden fear seeped out of me and was replaced by curiosity, wondering how it would feel to have her teeth sink into me.

Alexis's mouth lingered inches from mine. She smelled like the unliving but with a hint of cinnamon and spice. It was her magic.

The part of my brain that was working tried not to inhale, fearing one more deep breath of her pheromones would latch me to her unexpected seduction.

Leery, my eyes fluttered, disoriented by the power that loomed over my restless body. It was haunting, as if slipping into a nightmare rather than being awoken by one. Alexis wasn't herself and if I made the wrong move, it would be a lost battle in preventing her fangs from penetrating my flesh. No matter how confused I might be, I didn't want her biting me.

"I need you," she whispered, lips grazing my cheek.

I stared up at the ceiling, many thoughts forming but not one sticking. My body flushed, while my wolf paced like a rabid animal wanting to escape a vampire's control. My Omega didn't like feeling cornered and I needed to do something quick before I could no longer make the decisions.

Alexis's fingers curled and gripped my waist, possessively.

"Say yes to me just this once," she whispered in my ear, and I shuddered as her words touched a sensitive and fragile part of me that I thought was lost.

There was an aching plea, like an addict asking for one last hit. Slowly, I lifted my arm, pressing it atop Alexis's hand at my waist. I kept the center of my body immobile and avoided drawing attention to what I was doing.

"Rachelle. Look at me." It was a risk, but instinct told me no matter how tempting it was, she would never enthrall me. Granted, Rachelle wasn't herself but the way she held restraint so far told me I needed to trust in my gut.

"Look at me." There was brief hesitation, and I dreaded the outcome if I was wrong. But Rachelle's neck craned, eyes locked on mine, and I mentally sighed with relief. Cautious, trying not to startle her, I lifted my hand and brushed over the curve of her jaw.

The disquiet of her gaze placed regret into my heart. I should have tried harder to find and bring her home. As if the pain in her eyes was telling a story, I could see there was a lot she wanted to say and couldn't. What could be so damning that she'd leave, only to show up years later in such a drastic way? I wouldn't question her now. No. It would be pointless, and all I wanted was for her to find some peace.

I found myself falling deeper into her gaze. Not from compulsion, no. I was reliving our past because that's what she was doing. Something moist and warm slid down the side of my face to my ear and I found myself saying what I'd been convinced was not true.

"Fuck…" I shut my eyes and when I opened them again more tears released. We had something very special once and I missed it. "I still love you." I said the words so softly, dazed by my own admission.

It wasn't the kind of love that was fleeting. I'd given her my entire heart at one point, expecting a long life with her. It was foolish of me to think I could treat our past as just that. There was no mourning our life together or acceptance of her leaving me. I'd forced myself to go back to living with the hope of seeing her again in the back of my mind.

My sister had been right. The vampire witch who'd been raining havoc on everyone I cared about went from Alexis to Rachelle the moment our eyes reunited. How could I separate the two?

Rachelle's eyes changed colors, eventually softening into brown and I smiled. Her forehead pressed into mine, her possessive hand at my waist, tightening as if I were her only link to breathing. The tension between us was raw and powerful, magic swirling in and around us. The few inches of separation ended the instant Rachelle stretched all the way over me.

I could hardly take a breath without feeling lightheaded from the need searing my insides. Rachelle's lips neared mine and I groaned, pressing my hand against her chest, eyes squeezing tight, conflicted, and needful. My wolf cried inside and not for Rachelle, snapping me back to reality. What was I doing?

"I know. You are mated." Rachelle tried to hide the hurt, but I'd heard it. I expected her to retreat to her cold demeanor but instead she smiled. "There have been instances where a wolf could be tied to more than one mate. For many of the supernatural it isn't abnormal to love more than one. Wolves tend to be the ones always left behind, is all."

Was she seriously trying to convince me to be more open minded to loving two different people? I wanted to dismiss the notion but found it hard to open my mouth in defense. After all, that was me. The only issue was it would never work. They'd end up trying to kill each other before the night ended.

I gazed back at her and sighed. I couldn't focus with her on top and tapped her shoulder. One thing I loved about our relationship, I didn't have to say much for her to understand what I needed. And space was at the top of the list.

Once she moved off, I sat up, sliding my back against the headboard. I wouldn't say I was sexually frustrated, but I was damn close. I used every ounce of mental strength to not gaze at her lips.

One corner of her lip hinted at a smile, seeing through the emotional and physical barrier I had set in place.

"This is not funny." I was frustrated but more at myself.

Rachelle lifted both hands. "Fine. It isn't funny." She got up from the bed and frowned. "I know the part of you that is separate from your wolf still yearns for what we had."

I chose silence. What was I supposed to say? I knew the truth and she knew it too. Did I really have to say it aloud? My mind went back to Rikki, an ache forming in my chest. The words I promised Rikki were guzzling me up like a fresh kill. I had been blindly confident.

Comfortable silence fell between us until Rachelle opened the door. I watched; her gaze pointed in my direction but not on me. Her walls were coming back up and I found myself doing the same thing.

"I know you have questions that I can't answer at this time," she said. "But please, don't let that be the reason for not trusting me. At least, the part of me you know."

"You've changed," I said it softly, barely hearing my own words.

Rachelle stepped out of the room and before she closed the door, whispered, "No, I haven't. My darkness has always been there. It's just louder now."

I watched her shut the door and found myself crying. I'd broken down before, but this was different. My heart and soul were torn, and I couldn't pretend I was confident in my feelings anymore.

I lay on my side, pulling the pillow into myself, needing something to squeeze. I'd almost crossed a line and regret swallowed me whole. Rachelle was my Achilles heel that had crept back into my life. If she'd kissed me, I couldn't say I would have been able to resist.

By the time my tears ended, I'd finally fallen asleep.

Chapter Six

Morning came discreetly, sleeping inside a cave. Instead of waking up to an annoying alarm clock, I woke up to the eerie feeling of someone standing over me. Jaleel loomed over the bed, slit eyes not blinking. I shrieked, moving to one end, sitting up on my elbows, and bracing myself for an attack.

Discontented by Jaleel's proximity, I envisioned him sinking his sharp teeth into my flesh and draining me until I was as dry as a raisin. My wolf screamed to get away. If Jaleel smelled my anxiety, he didn't acknowledge it.

He was in his natural form, rough scaly skin, black slitted eyes, and pointy teeth. I preferred the various faces he shifted to when he wanted to appear human. I turned away briefly, finding my judgement of him to be harsh. Granted, he deserved no respect from me after kidnapping my brother all to keep his master happy, but he'd been different since I arrived. Not that he liked me, but he held more value than I originally accredited him.

Last night, I knew his main reason for helping me when Rachelle entered my room was to protect her emotional wellbeing. He knew if she hurt me, it would tear her apart. But he wasn't fooling anyone. There was a sincere intention directed my way. Though I deemed his past actions as unjustifiable, there were reasons unknown to me that gave him cause to act gruesomely when taunting me for weeks and taking my brother.

"Will you stop gawking at me?" Jaleel's tongue slithered through his lips.

I smiled. He wasn't looking at me like dinner on a plate anymore. He played with a quarter, dancing it between his fingers, waiting for me to get up.

"You like me!" I don't know why I felt the need to say it but if I was going to have to put up with seeing him, the least I could do was make my time around him bearable.

He had no brows or facial cues for me to read his reaction.

"The only thing I like about you is how succulent you'd taste."

A thick lump formed in my throat, and I didn't allow myself to picture that. Instead, I slid out of bed pretending his presence wasn't unnerving. He took two steps back, and I let out my breath.

Leaving the fear out of my tone, I asked, fumbling to put on my shoes, "Is there a reason I'm up?"

"You have 15 minutes to be ready to leave." Jaleel's disdain was noted.

I felt the same way. I waited for him to say more but his haunting glare was all I got.

"A task?"

"Food has been prepared. Use your nose to find it and I will meet you there." Jaleel saw my protest but left before a word could escape my lips.

I wasn't going to push my luck by sneaking around. I reached the dining hall and suspected there were eyes on me even if I couldn't see anyone. I ate quickly, suspecting Jaleel wouldn't let me finish my meal once he arrived.

Jaleel came into the hall, human features replacing any trace of him being a reptilian vympyrus. He stood an even six feet, with brown shaggy hair and green eyes. His impassive stare made me wonder if he was ever human.

"If you stare any harder, I might assume you have interest in me too."

My eyes turned back to the food on the table. I grabbed another piece of bacon, taking a bite.

"Where is..."

"She is indisposed." Jaleel turned, expecting me to follow.

I was new to the supernatural world, but I wasn't naïve.

"She's a vampire and witch and you're telling me she's susceptible to illness?"

Jaleel lips curled. "If you were a smart wolf, you'd stop pestering me."

I took it he didn't like being asked questions. Though I knew he would never lay a finger on me, I didn't put it past him to seek out one of my loved ones to harm. So yes, I was a smart wolf and learned during my first few weeks as a werewolf when to keep my mouth shut. I remembered antagonizing a werewolf in a bar I frequented before learning it had been a werewolf bar the entire time. That wolf had hit me so hard, snapping my collarbone like a skinny twig.

Jaleel kept a distance, but it felt like he was standing right over me, micromanaging every bite I took. I looked down at my plate with one pancake left and sighed. I was hungry but if Jaleel stared any harder it might disappear before I had the chance to eat it.

I stood, grabbing the pancake and waved it to signal I was ready to go.

Jaleel grumbled underneath his breath and walked off. His stride was swift. I had to skip a few steps to catch up, stuffing the pancake into my mouth. This partnership was off to a great start.

*

The exit had been easier than expected. There was no wide opening that led us to the outside world. Instead, I'd been guided through a door, unable to see to the other side. Jaleel stepped through and he vanished. It was like he'd been swallowed by darkness. I didn't think this was a trap, waving my hand near the door.

I screamed when rough scaly fingers locked around my wrist and pulled me through. I landed on my knees; my stomach queasy as if I'd been spinning in circles. I closed my eyes and vomit raised to the base of my throat.

"Weakling," Jaleel grumbled.

I couldn't lift my head up yet, but my hand could do just fine. I stuck my middle finger out at Jaleel and took a slow breath, hunched on all fours.

My fingers dug into grass, a cool breeze brushing over the back of my neck. I sat on my knees and looked around. We were at Washington Park in Portland. Joggers were running along the trail; we stood on the island of grass where people tended to have picnics. It was calm and quiet, too early for most people.

One day in the cave felt like several and I cherished having the sun on my skin. It was a rare occasion to have this much warmth in late November. I liked Portland. The stereotype of Portland being a unique place to live wasn't far-fetched. They had everything between the World Naked Bike Ride event to a person walking a pig down the street like a dog on a leash.

Before my life had taken a turn, I'd visited Portland often, but something always kept me closer to Salem. It was quieter and less dramatic. But there was quiet and then there was quieter and that was Mill City which was more like a town. It made sense for Rikki and the pack to be huddled there. Less chance of being discovered. I'd moved to Mill City because of the asshole who decided to attack me that fateful and memorable night. The transition had been hectic, a string of raw emotions flaring out of me.

Sitting on my knees, I hadn't truly realized how much I missed my home with Rikki until now. Yes, I missed my mate and the pack but Mill City... I hadn't thought too much about it. I missed the trees, mountains, and the stream flowing throughout the town. I missed sitting outside on the back porch and staring up at the night sky with my pack. Granted, I hated cougars, but I reminded myself that I was a werewolf every time I could sense one.

"Are you done daydreaming?" Jaleel's hissing tone was enough to remind me exactly where I was. "You are drawing attention to us."

I glanced around. Several people pretended to mind their own business, but I saw their sideways glances.

Casually, I stood, grass already staining my washout jeans. I was outside and if I wanted to, I could try to run but what would be the point. I chose to stay, and I had to follow through with that. My wolf wanted to fight but I knew better. There was no escaping Jaleel and trying would only piss him off and probably give him an appetite. You didn't run from predators. Running only delayed the inevitable. In the end, you'd always end up fighting anyway.

Settling on the fact that I would be stuck with Jaleel, I sighed. I bit the bottom of my lip and contemplated if it was worth asking questions. Jaleel was great at not answering.

His head slanted enough to make me notice him watching me.

"Don't talk."

That left me with more questions. I glanced around searching for what was about to happen. We were at the center of the park with no privacy, people walking along the trail. But then something seemed to change. I noticed one man running, who'd noticed us but stopped as if we'd done something extreme. He looked our way, eyes darting everywhere as if searching for us. I could see the temptation to come closer, but he decided to stay put before running in the opposite direction.

"The vermin can no longer see us," Jaleel confirmed. "But seems your species can." He looked toward the dog staring straight at me while his owner drank from her bottled water.

He was comparing me to a dog. Great. I looked forward to his next insult. And like Amber, he had regarded humans as vermin. I was beginning to think it was vampire slang. Before I could come up with something witty, a chill ran up my spine. Someone was here. My chest tightened and I let my fingertips form into claws without meaning too. Fear leaked out of me, and I sucked in a breath, reminding myself I was more than human. I was stronger than I was even a week ago. I wouldn't be foolish enough to believe I could take on whatever *being,* made my insides squirm as if bugs were crawling in me, but I wouldn't go down without a fight.

"Do not show yourself to be a threat," Jaleel sneered. "And unless you want him to have a taste, stop spraying your fear all over the place."

My brows kneaded together, ready to say my two cents but I was working on keeping my mouth shut. I didn't know who we were meeting but based on the power I felt, it was enough for me to shut up.

"Ah. You bring me a gift." Someone whispered softly in my ear, and I turned, expecting him to be standing behind me.

Teeth gritted; I was relieved to find no one.

"My patience is not one to waste today." Jaleel's face skewed into a deep frown.

"As usual, you are no fun." Whoever Jaleel was talking to took comedy lessons.

A butterfly flew just above my head and Jaleel shook his head out of annoyance. Before I could say anything, the butterfly turned to mist, blurring my vision as it reshaped into a human. Brown eyes locked onto me, and I averted mine before whoever this was tried to spell me. The stunning androgynous person's eyes closed and when they opened again, the pupils were the shade of purple lollipops.

A hand stretched out for me, and I found myself swayed by the magic pulsating from this stranger. Their eyes lingered on me, intense and seductive but discreet. Jaleel either didn't notice or didn't care what was happening.

"I am Fenix." Their smile widened when I continued to stand there dazed and flustered. Their features were soft and curved like a woman's, with thick brows and an intense stare that showcased a masculine side.

I had to shake my head to wake myself from the snare Fenix placed. I thought better of it and decided not to shake their hand.

"Fenix is a vampire Fae," Jaleel explained. "They aren't going to harm you."

I caught onto the pronouns and nodded, relieved I hadn't been presumptuous. Fenix's lips pursed into a mischievous grin when I didn't reach out to shake their hand.

"I'm a Paramedic. We tend not to shake people's hands. Germs. Scabies. Sweat."

I smiled back, faking it.

Fenix's eyes shifted toward Jaleel and chuckled.

"I see why Alexis let you bring her."

Jaleel sneered.

"Yes!" Fenix leaned close to Jaleel, mockingly. "I know who she is. Nothing gets past me." They leaned back as if they hadn't already checked me out. Fenix stood my height, average build, wearing only a V-neck gold silk vest and jeans. Their hair was slicked back and cut short at the neck. "I'm surprised Alexis hasn't bitten you yet."

"I'm not hers to bite." I wasn't a fan of being scrutinized. "I'm mated to—"

Fenix waved their hand out nonchalantly.

"Oh, I know. Your Alpha has been stirring up a lot of trouble to get you back. Word is, you went to Alexis willingly. Is that true?"

Somehow, I knew my answer mattered. I glanced at Jaleel who didn't bother looking at me, but I could see in the way his jaw tightened that I needed to answer and give the right one. I could mention how they pretty much left me with no choice, but I wouldn't do that. In the end, I had made the decision to leave with Jaleel and stay with Alexis even after Rikki asked me to come back.

"I have chosen to stay by Alexis's side, for now," I answered.

Fenix just nodded once. "And... how do you know Alexis?"

I wasn't sure if this was a trick question and decided not to answer right away.

"I thought you knew everything," I said.

"Point to you," Fenix whispered. A long breath passed before Fenix spoke again. "She does smell ripe!" Fenix was clearly talking about me. "Like a peach, sweet and soft, right before you take a bite."

Jaleel made a point of shifting closer to me. I stared between the two, confused. Were my eyes deceiving me or was Jaleel protecting me?

"She will be claimed. She has already chosen to stay by my sire's side."

"I'm not—"

Jaleel's eyes darted to mine briefly, but long enough to shut my mouth.

Fenix only studied me before responding to Jaleel. There was much control in the way Fenix stood, casual but purposeful, as if waiting for Jaleel to make the first move.

"It is my Queen's birthright to have what is owed to her." They looked at me. "If you are being forced to stay, you can always take shelter with me. Just say the word."

Something told me I didn't want to go anywhere with Fenix, however nice they appeared to be.

"I'm good," I said.

"Tell your sire not to make this harder than it needs to be," Fenix said.

"I'll take your advice into consideration." Jaleel only stared down at Fenix with a gaze hungry for violence. "But, for now, just know she is under my sire's protection, and you'll never know what she tastes like. At least not before me."

Was he joking? I had to look at Jaleel to make sure he was but of course, I couldn't read anything. I'd remind him I was off limits after we left.

Fenix held Jaleel's gaze uncomfortably long before nodding their head.

"Wow." They took a step back, then clapped and began cackling as if they'd accepted something. Their eyes lit up, crimson tears streaming down the side of their face, laughter shaking their body. What the hell was so funny? The sound was deep and sinister, and I now pictured Fenix eating children. The soft way they smiled no longer showed gentleness but a deranged sociopath counting the days until they'd get to go hunting.

I stared, dumbfounded by how easily they'd switched their demeanor. I was officially freaked out and needed answers. What the hell was going on?

"Until next time," Fenix bowed their head and misted before flying away as a butterfly.

My mouth hung open, shocked and confused. I knew Jaleel wouldn't explain anything, but I had to try and get answers.

"Who is Alexis protecting me from?" I asked.

Jaleel ignored me and I snarled.

I was over his dismissive behavior and wasn't going to let this go until I got answers. When he tried to walk away, I reached out and grabbed his arm.

He turned so fast, like a snake about to bite. His eyes latched onto mine; head craned as he hunched down.

"Perhaps you are getting too comfortable and forgetting what I am."

I squeezed my fist tightly and waited for him to attack me.

Instead, he looked past me. I thought he was only choosing to ignore me again, but I heard footsteps. Jaleel smiled and I turned to see a woman approaching. Clearly, we were back to being visible.

The woman looked to be in her mid-twenties, frightful green eyes staring with inner conflict. She was aware that she wasn't in control of her own actions and when she looked at me, I saw a plea. She looked fragile and small next to Jaleel's tall and muscular body. The woman wore jogging pants and had her earbuds on, but she'd walked over here as if she'd been out on a prowl.

Jaleel's human features were impressive but that still didn't make sense for a woman to melt so easily after seeing him from a distance.

"What is your name?" Jaleel asked.

The woman looked entranced and stopped short of his reach.

"Jennifer."

"Mm." Jaleel offered out his hand. "A pretty name for a pretty woman." Jaleel looked at me briefly and I realized what he was doing.

"Okay, I get the point." Whatever he was doing, I wanted him to stop.

Jaleel continued. "Jennifer. I must be honest. I called you over to punish someone. You want to help me with that?"

She looked scared and I could tell she didn't want to do this, but his compulsion was too strong. When she nodded, I saw tears swelling around her eyes.

"Jaleel. Stop this," I muttered. Jaleel ignored me and I moved to pull her away, but he was fast, turning her to face me with the woman's back against his chest. "Please. I get it now," I begged. I couldn't have this woman die because of me.

"You draw too much attention, I'll have to kill every person in this park," Jaleel warned.

My heart raced and I felt nausea at the thought of her being killed. I had to believe he wouldn't kill her.

His arms snaked around the woman's waist possessively and my heart sank low into my chest.

"You smell..." Jaleel took a deep breath and smiled. "Delicious," he finished. He guided his nose along the curve of the woman's neck and to anyone watching, they would look like two lovers embracing. "Do not scream but I want you to beg. Beg me to stop. And when I don't, look into that woman's eyes and remember, she did this to you."

He teased her neck and she cried and all I could do was stand there. He was stronger and faster, and I couldn't risk him bluffing to kill everyone if I did anything. I shouldn't have felt guilty, but I did. But more than that, I felt angry that he'd use this moment as an excuse to be cruel. He was taking away her consent. I wanted to call him every name I could think of, but I knew he'd only punish her for it, so I stayed silent.

Then he did it. His fangs lengthened and his tongue grazed her neck; she shuddered. When his fangs sank inside her flesh she groaned and begged, all while looking at me. Blood drizzled out, escaping from his mouth as he fed on her blood. He was draining her right here in the park, and no one noticed.

When he finished, I watched him sink his fangs into his tongue to brush his blood over the two holes in her neck. He let her go and I stared as the fang bites disappeared. Jaleel turned her around, the woman's eyes red from tears.

"You were running and then got very tired. You never met me or her." Jaleel's eyes met mine briefly. "Go home and rest. You deserve a day off." When he let go of the woman, she walked away with no sign of the traumatic experience she'd endured.

I wouldn't waste my breath telling Jaleel what I thought of him at that moment. He wanted me to see him as a monster to fear. The fact that he'd gone out his way to show such cruelty was enough to see he wasn't as evil as he wanted me to believe. I'd learned a long time ago, the ones that showed off were always the weakest in the mind.

No. I wouldn't entertain his actions.

"I want to speak to Alexis," I said.

Jaleel studied me. He'd expected me to react, and my dismissal had puzzled him.

"Why?"

I shrugged. "I see no point in me being here with you. You showed me off to the vampire Fae. My jobs done, right?"

"What is your game?" Jaleel questioned.

I snorted. "That's your problem. You're the only one playing." I shifted and waved my arm. "Are we close to the magic door, or will we just pop back into the cave with the snap of your finger?"

Jaleel sneered and brushed past me, vanishing after he'd taken a few more steps. One second he was there, and the next he was gone.

"Uh, fuck." I turned and walked in the same direct path he'd gone, and just when I thought I'd taken a misguided step, my skin flushed, stomach swirling as I staggered, finding myself pressed into a wall. I was swallowed into dim candlelight and groaned, sucking in a breath. I was back in the cave.

Chapter Seven

Jaleel was nowhere to be found when I was back in the cave, and I sighed.

"Bastard." I turned and leaned my back against the wall, trying to catch my breath. I was not a fan of portals and hoped to avoid them in the future. Sweat trickled down my brow; I was exhausted as if I'd been running miles. Jaleel wanted to make me angry, and he'd succeeded. It was unlike me to give someone what they wanted.

"Where is Braelin?"

I lifted my head to find Malcom standing next to an archway, a smile lifting the corner of his mouth. I let out a sharp breath, leaned forward and stood on two wobbly legs, pleading with them not to give out.

There was a shift in the air when he could see Braelin wasn't going to pop up anytime soon. He'd spent the rest of the night waiting for us to return and no one bothered to mention Braelin leaving. I felt crappy since I should have reached out to him last night.

"She's gone."

His eyes opened wide, and fear clamped his jaw shut.

I realized how that sounded and walked up to him.

"That came out wrong. She's fine."

He let out a relieved breath.

I knew I should explain but I also needed to sit and drink something cold. There was tension in my shoulders, my body jittery from going through a portal.

Malcolm could tell I needed a moment, brows kneading together.

"Portal traveling can be a lot to handle in the beginning and unfortunately, Jaleel only adds to the stress."

I chuckled. "You think?"

"This way."

I recognized where we were and moved to the fireplace to keep warm when we got to where he'd wanted to take me. I crouched down and moved my hands close to the flames. The wind whistled around the space I assumed was Malcolm's personal living quarters. The last time I'd been here was when I first met him, inches from falling off the cliff.

It was still difficult to call him my father, a word I hadn't used in years since the man who raised me had passed. He'd been everything to me and knowing the truth now wouldn't change that.

Malcolm held out a bottle of water and offered me a smile when I took it. He took a step back and stood at an awkward distance, doing his best to not pressure me.

I consumed most of the water and placed it to my side, deciding to get comfortable and sit. That seemed to relax Malcolm enough to do the same. The quiet gave me a moment to work up enough courage to speak. I chose a less personal topic, not eager to share anything about me.

"As you witnessed, Braelin is very protective of me."

"She loves you," Malcom responded.

I nodded. I thought back to the night I met her and how devoted she was to finding me. I guess that's why it was so easy for me to open up to her when it usually took much longer.

"I love her too." I pressed my knees into my chest and curled my arms around them, hugging myself. I sometimes wondered how I made it this far without having her in my life when I was a little girl who wanted someone to look up to. "She loves so hard. I knew she'd continue to pick fights with Alexis and that's why I had to get her to leave."

Malcolm's somber expression grew into one of sadness. He'd wanted more time with Braelin, not confident he'd see her again.

"She was going to get herself killed. And I would have continued to walk on eggshells here if she'd stayed." I looked at him. "I need to face this."

"Alone." He knew what I hadn't said aloud.

"That's not what I mean." Closing my eyes, I let myself listen to the crackling of the fire, not in a rush to explain. Maybe in some ways, it was what I meant. I couldn't rely on others to help me figure out how to let Alexis go. We had a past outside of everyone. Before I'd known anyone else. "Rachelle. Alexis. She's one and the same for me. And despite your history with her and what she's done to get my attention, I need to…" I paused, sorting through my words. I wasn't comfortable saying it aloud to him. "Figure some things out."

Malcolm sighed and stared off into the fire. "She won't let you go."

"Something's wrong with her." I found myself whispering, too many loyal servants of Alexis most likely listening in.

Malcolm didn't speak but his eyes said as much.

"If I'd left with Rikki, I would have regretted it and my mate would have stood by my side, doubting if I'd moved on."

"A mate bond is forever. Only death can separate you from each other." Malcolm's eyes narrowed on the fire.

I knew what being mated meant and I had to bite down on my words not to react emotionally. Rikki and I had been through a lot in a short time, our love as genuine and honest as the oxygen flowing into me now.

Rachelle was my past, or at least I thought, and that made this a painful reminder of how messy my life had become in a matter of hours. I loved Rachelle and at one point she'd meant everything to me. She supported me through tough times. Encouraged and loved me without question. How could I treat those memories like a mild fling?

I wanted to be understood and not be judged on how I felt about Rachelle. It was mostly memories that left me feeding from the past and it wasn't easy to shut off. Those memories kept replaying in my mind and I didn't think I'd be able to leave until I went through the stages of grief I'd only tucked away. It didn't mean I was considering going back to her. My life with Rikki was something I wanted to keep. Rikki had given me something even Rachelle couldn't provide me with and that was security. I knew I could screw up and she'd still love me despite of that. She saw me as an equal and one who contributed to her life. She still had a past I was naïve to, but I trusted that she would tell me when she was ready. We'd only been together for a short time but even now I knew she wouldn't let anyone force her to leave my side.

No, I'd been the one to do that. Maybe in the beginning, my reasons for leaving with Jaleel were the right choice but what could I say about now? Part of me questioned if I deserved someone as loyal as Rikki. She'd wait for me but that didn't make me feel good about myself.

I needed to find a way to let Rachelle go. I could still love her without her having her effect on me. But was I making the right decision? That was beginning to eat at me.

I twisted the water bottle in circles, needing to do something with my hands.

"You loved her?" I asked.

Malcolm's head lifted and I could see that he'd been wanting to share something with me and waiting.

"Your mother was my mate. I'll never feel that way for someone again."

I'd been vague on who I was talking about, still thinking about my own issues.

"Not her." I smiled, wanting him to see that his words meant a lot. "I was referring to my mom and Braelin's mother. Did you love… her?"

Malcolm's eyes widened and I could tell he hadn't spoken about her in a long time. I could detect the change in his heart rate, beating fast as he leaned back and stared off to the side. He arched his back, and I heard a pop.

"She…she didn't get the chance to really shine the way she deserved. Our marriage was the one thing that kept me feeling worth a damn. She knew how to keep me on my toes, and she was an amazing mother. I cherished every moment with her and wouldn't change a thing."

"That's how I feel about Rachelle. The difference between you and me is my first love isn't gone and I never wanted her to leave me."

He nodded, understanding my conflict. "I'll support you no matter what." His support didn't matter to me much, but I appreciated the intent behind his words. "If I were in your shoes, this would be hard for me too. But there are other ways of moving on that don't require you staying here."

And there was that tug of regret again. I frowned, staring at the flames dying down. I thought of the crack in Alexis's demeanor the previous night and knew my answer.

"If this was only about letting go of the past then I would have left with Rikki whether Rachelle threatened to torment my pack or not. I can't leave her the way she is. And I choose to believe that she has more good inside her than darkness. It's because of our past that I will find her again; the truth is, I want her to be happy. To live and maybe find someone else to love again. I know if I leave her now, the evil everyone truly fears from her will be real and permanent."

Footsteps approached the entranceway, and I looked up to find Arlana standing with a grin on her face.

"Bonding with your father. How adorable?"

I rolled my eyes but didn't say anything.

"You should go." Malcolm encouraged. He wanted to be alone. I noticed his shoulders bunched in and rigid like he'd been holding his wolf back and was losing the battle.

My skin flushed from the sound of a scream, sharp and horrid. Claws protruded from my fingers and my jaw snapped, a shift being nearly forced out. The smell of blood was strong as if I'd been bathed in it.

Arlana moved too fast down the corridor and was out of sight before I had time to register what was happening.

"We should—"

"If you think for one minute I'm going to stay here, you are about to get a good lesson on the kind of person I am." I moved through the hall, instinct guiding me to where blood had been spilled. I could hear snarls and the clicking of metal smashing against metal, shivers rushing up my arms. A power I'd never felt slammed into my chest, and I stopped just around the corner.

I wasn't a skillful fighter, but Tato had been teaching me and I knew enough to know my limit. But when I turned the corner, everything I envisioned being capable of was demolished.

Magic shot out from a woman's hands in bright colors of blue and white, manifesting into a sword. She held it as if it weighed nothing and swung it, slicing off a vampire's arm. She spoke an unrecognizable language and seconds later what looked like an orb hovered over the palm of her hands.

Arlana held two daggers, leaping towards another woman with a magic sword who was now finishing the vampire off with a deadly move that sent the vampire's head flying off his shoulders.

We were in the main hall where Rikki had come the previous night, over two dozen fighting with weapons and magic.

I turned and found a woman holding a crossbow aimed at me. She smirked and I could hear her finger press into the trigger.

My wolf's instincts slammed against my skull, shaking me alert. Panic clogged my lungs, an unfathomable feeling of defeat and fear burning inside when I realized I couldn't move. Magic held me in place as if I'd been super glued into that position. Something fast came shooting my way but before it could hit me, Malcolm leaped in front of me, taking the blow.

I screamed, expecting to find Malcolm drop to the floor with a hole in his chest, but he just staggered, leaning against me. That seemed to be all I needed to break the magic holding me just in time to have him collapse into my arms.

He turned onto his back, a dart sticking in his chest but was breathing and very much alive.

The thought of losing him before I had the chance to get to know him was the wakeup call I needed to fight. I tilted my head, watching the woman load another dart into the crossbow and growled with my teeth bared. Werewolf translation: I was pissed as fuck. I wouldn't let Malcolm risk his life for me like that again. Braelin needed him a lot more than I did.

Just as the woman aimed for me again, I ran straight for her, leaping onto my hands as if I had shifted to my wolf, on all fours, the dart shooting over my head. When I leapt off my legs, I propelled off the ground, slamming my weight into her side. Air heaved out of her lungs as I knocked her to the ground and landed on top. She reached for a weapon tucked in her jacket and I pinned her arm in place, relieved I was stronger. My claws were thick and sharp on my human shaped hands, but I snarled instead of doing something I wouldn't be able to take back. I wasn't a killer and I'd keep it that way for as long as I lived. Perhaps it was my human thoughts running my moral compass, but I preferred never to be put to an ultimate test of *what do I do, if?*

I knew I couldn't let her go since she'd only reach for her weapons again. My hesitation had been too long, giving someone the perfect opportunity to sneak up on me. Someone came from behind and something thin and silver curled around my neck as they jerked my head back.

My fingers tried peeling the thin silver chain from around my neck, but it was no use as it cut into my skin, searing me. I let out a chocking cry as the woman under me, arms free, reached for her dagger.

I had to make a choice. Free the chain around me or stop the woman under me from getting to her weapon. There was a split second where I felt my mind slip away, on the verge of blacking out. My wolf was about to take control and put my human consciousness to sleep.

My neck burned, heart rate sped, and lungs gasped for air but that wouldn't matter if they killed me. I wouldn't matter and Rikki would mourn not being here to save me.

Save yourself.

My eyes widened from the voice that whispered in my head. I hadn't realized my eyes were closed and now I was very much aware of the seconds I had before I was killed. I squeezed my thighs into the woman as the person behind me tried dragging me off.

"Fucking quit resisting and we won't have to hurt you!" It was a woman who'd been behind me as she screamed in my ear, hurriedly.

The woman below found her dagger. I snarled raggedly and caught her arm just in time as she tried to stab me in the stomach. I struggled to keep the dagger from piercing into my flesh and had nearly succeeded in fighting the woman off when the one behind me tightened her grip around my neck, lifting me up a few inches.

I wasn't as quick to stop the woman this time and she drove the dagger into my lower belly. Something warm spilled out of me, a burning furious pain causing my body to stiffen.

Kill them. We need to kill them.

My eyes widened. That voice was the shock to the system I needed to fight harder. But to kill. That wasn't me.

I closed my eyes and gave into my wolf a bit more and reached behind me, my claws digging into the woman's arms.

She hissed and I dug deeper, raking my claws down her arms to her wrists and she let go.

I had maybe a few seconds to act and looked down as the woman below moved to drive the dagger into me again. This time I was ready and caught her wrist with both hands, peeling her fingers open to rip the dagger away.

I punched her in the face and flung the weapon across the room. I could barely breathe from the amount of force the woman had with the chain around my neck, but I didn't have time to think about how to breathe. My eyes watered, tears slipping out and blurring my vision, but I could see someone coming for me. A man this time.

His eyes were violet as he sneered at me. He grabbed me by the hair, trying to drag me off and I twisted awkwardly just as he stopped.

I expected him to land a deadly blow but there was nothing. Unsure, I looked up, laying on my side at a weird angle to find the man standing over me no longer with a head.

Blood spurted from what was left of him and onto me. I glanced around and found Alexis standing a few feet from me with a sword in hand. She looked flawless and elegant which made me shake my head in astonishment. How could someone so deadly look like that while holding a bloody edged sword she had just used to cut off someone's head?

My paramedic abilities wouldn't be saving this guy.

I scooted backward and pressed my hand against my side where I'd been stabbed as I watched Alexis go to town on a few more unknown individuals.

I expected her to kill them all, but she just stopped.

Jaleel walked over to Alexis, blood dripping from his clawed fingers. He looked calm and unruffled from the attack.

There were a lot of dead people around us. For me it was a lot but probably for Alexis this was nothing. Seven people lay unmoving and without any signs of living.

There were several individuals backing toward the cave exit, some hunched over in pain.

One woman stepped forward, taking the position as lead. Her white hair fell around her face, eyes creased hard and angled at Alexis.

"My Queen will give you this moment as a warning. Give back her inheritance or we will come back with too many for even you to cut through."

"I don't acknowledge this as a threat." Alexis held the sword at eye level as if it weighed nothing and then lowered her hand as the sword hovered in place. She smiled and the sword moved quickly, the woman pivoting to the side and barely dodging the sword. "But…you are free to come again."

The white-haired woman scowled and faced Alexis again, her tone even tempered.

"You will have to do a lot better than that."

Alexis smiled and I shifted a glance to where the sword landed.

My eyes widened, realizing the sword now pierced through the chest of the woman who'd stabbed me in the stomach. The sword had slammed through her harshly enough to penetrate the stone wall, pinning her in place. Blood poured out from the corner of the woman's mouth. She was dead. The other woman who'd been chocking me was also dead, not too far from Jaleel.

The white-haired woman turned to see one of her friends dead but when she turned back her expression was blank. Instead of looking at Alexis, she gazed at me and smiled before disappearing.

I shifted nervously, expecting the woman to magically reappear, my eyes darting everywhere, trying to listen for feet shuffling closer. When she didn't come for me, I looked back to where I last saw her and saw the others with her vanish into thin air.

Alexis sneered. "Fucking Faes!" Then she was pressed into my side, lifting me from the ground and carrying me.

I grimaced and screamed from the unexpected movement. I didn't realize I was in so much pain until she moved me.

"Get a fucking healer, now!" Alexis called out as my vision suddenly darkened.

I should have been healing by now. My head jolted back and gasped when I felt my shirt being torn open.

I was now laying stretched out on a hard padded surface. My skin felt sticky and wet, and I shivered as my eyes rolled to the back of my head.

I wondered if this was the part where I saw the light right before dying. Hands pressed against my flesh, and I writhed, suddenly feeling like my insides were being dissected.

My wolf was crying, and I couldn't do anything to stop the pain from happening. My mind went to the only place I could think of. My happy place, surrounded by trees.

My wolf had caught a new game. It was one of my morning routines to have time to myself. I loved my pack and knew they'd be waiting for me to head back soon. I never felt so loved before until I joined them. Yes, I resisted at first but only because I was afraid of loving them too much only to lose them.

As I woke up, Rikki stood over me, holding out my clothes. She was always there after those moments. Reminding me of where I belonged. In her arms.

Now, I whispered her name. I needed my mate but feared this time she would not be able to come.

Chapter Eight

I awoke to the sound of someone whispering with enough hostility to make me concerned. My eyes rolled around underneath my lids, resisting the urge to fall back asleep. My head pounded, the front of it aching as if I was recovering from a concussion.

"She's waking up." Malcolm spoke low in my ear, and I felt lips brushing over my forehead. "You're going to be fine." I could hear his relief as if he hadn't been too certain moments ago.

Anger, regret, and a mix of more emotions I couldn't break down came in the form of a body, warm hands cupping my cheek. I didn't need to open my eyes to know who it was, tears gathering and nearly releasing.

"Rikki!"

Her fingers combed my hair, and I relaxed under her touch.

"I'm here."

I let out a breath, not expecting her to be real. I was too weak to sit up or I would've leapt into her arms. I hadn't realized I was crying until Rikki's thumbs swiped tears away.

Rikki kissed both sides of my face, hovering close, her skin hot and dry. Her wolf was burning to come out and protect me. The amount of control she had wouldn't last, needing to make sure I was safe, and in her arms, far away from Alexis and her number two, Jaleel.

It took me time to adjust to my surroundings and notice who was in the room. Rikki sat beside me with my father on the other side, close but hesitant to lean in.

My head hurt less but if I didn't eat and shift, I wouldn't get better any time soon.

Alexis stood in the far corner of the room, her back turned to me. She was stiff and unmoving and if I hadn't known she was a vampire I would have been concerned since she wasn't breathing. Her energy was all sorts of wrong, like she'd been splintered and shredded, left with only an empty shell of a body.

"I am done playing your game. Bonnie is coming home with me." Rikki was near her breaking point, not giving me room to speak. "And before you argue with me about staying here out of fear of her retaliation or trying to save what humanity she has left, just know that our pack needs you more than she does."

Her words stung, leaving me stupefied. I hadn't expected Rikki to say that, and it left me breathless. For the past several hours I had contemplated if I was making the right decision but hearing Rikki call me out on my own bullshit was enough to make me realize I'd been here too long, and it had only been two days.

Did I deserve to be the pack's Omega when I'd bailed on them for Alexis? In the beginning it made sense to go but the moment I knew who Alexis was, I knew she was never going to hurt me or my pack. I could have left.

"She will not last under your care." Alexis's voice was low and hostile.

Rikki's jaw tightened and I could hear her teeth grinding together.

"Is that so?" Rikki's body shifted, heat blazing from her skin. She spoke through a sneer like she was choking on anger. "Last I checked, my mate was nearly killed under your care."

"You don't know who your enemies are so how will you protect her? From whom?" Alexis turned and glared at Rikki with curiosity and casual calmness, the eerie tension in her shoulders gone. "She is alive despite what happened. And they weren't trying to kill her."

I was tired of them discussing me as if my opinion didn't matter.

"If you both could cool off in your corners, I'd like to say something."

"What do you mean they weren't trying to kill her?" Rikki hadn't overlooked Alexis's words and ignored me.

Alexis didn't say anything for a long time and that was enough to make me more concerned than I originally thought to be. She licked her lips as if deciding what to say. She was working up a story and if I didn't recognize the glare in her eyes, I wouldn't have known the truths she was going to try and keep out. My instinct was screaming that she was going to give us only pieces of the story.

I wanted to jump out of bed and shake the damn truth out of her, but I was still weak. Figuring I had enough strength to at least slide to the edge of the bed, I moved slowly, flicking my hand out to stop Rikki from helping. I wasn't fragile or someone who needed help with every step I took.

Rikki saw my determination and anger, taking a step back. She'd gotten my message loud and clear.

When I made it to where I wanted to be, legs draped off the bed, I stared up at Alexis waiting for her to look at me. Her eyes met mine and I knew she was silently pleading for me to stay. I could. But then it would be me truly choosing her over my mate. Over my pack. I wanted to be here and bring back the woman I once put above all others. But it wasn't my job to save her, and I wouldn't put her above keeping my pack safe.

"I will always choose to believe you aren't as cruel as you act like you are. You think pissing Rikki off with ghouls and threatening to harm members of my pack is what kept me staying but it was more than that. It was me…me needing to save you. But I can't and it would be for my own selfish reasons more than anything. But I want you to try for you."

I let out a shaky breath, surprised she'd been listening this long.

"But please know, I want to see you happy and exist outside of this cave. I'll always cherish what we had. That won't change. You are my first love and were my best friend."

Whatever control Alexis had was slowly crumbling and the corner of her eye twitched, reacting to my words. She needed to hear me say that and maybe it was the first step to letting go, for both of us.

I smiled. "For them, you're Alexis. But for me, you'll always be…Rachelle. All I ask is that you give yourself some grace and let them see you aren't the threat, at least not anymore."

For the first time, I watched as Rachelle's chest raise, taking a breath. Vampires didn't need to breathe, but I suspected she was feeling human for the first time in a long time. When a tear fell from her eyes, dark and crimson, I knew she'd be okay. Maybe she still didn't believe that, but I knew in time she would.

I looked at her and saw her. The woman who taught me what it meant to be loved. Rachelle huffed. "You've always reminded me of her."

I frowned. "My mother?" I asked.

Rachelle turned to wipe her crimson tears away before facing me again.

"In ways, but that's not who I meant."

"Then who?" Rikki didn't sound pissed off anymore and that was a good sign.

Rachelle surprised me again, answering her without a displeased tone.

"Your grandmother." Rachelle pursed her lips as if deciding what to say next. "Your bloodline is rich with history and power. Your grandmother was a lot like you. Smart, sarcastic, passionate, and she had no issue of reminding me of my place."

Her eyes glittered and I could see it.

"You loved her too?" I guessed.

Her eyes widened, staggered that I'd noticed. She looked at Jaleel whose expression hadn't changed this entire time.

"She's the reason I was cursed and cast from my coven," she said.

Now it was my turn to look shocked, mouth parted.

"Ugh." What did one say to that?

"Bonnie's grandmother is the one you fell in love with and were forbidden to see?" It was Rikki's turn to speak, jumping right in with her conclusion.

Rachelle nodded once. "Almost 400 years ago I was merely a black witch who was sent to guard and protect your grandmother from her fate passed down from generation to generation." Rachelle licked her lips and I noticed how she always tried masking her face right after.

"You're hungry?" I questioned.

Her eyes widened. "Am I that obvious?"

I nodded.

"Perhaps, we're both hungry," she said.

Jaleel nodded. "I'll make sure food is ready by the time you all make it down." He vanished a second later.

"Shall we?" Rachelle asked, waving toward the door.

I nodded. This time when Rikki tried to help, I didn't turn her away. I took the hand offered and felt her do most of the work, lifting me to my feet.

Rachelle kept her eyes on Rikki's fingers laced through mine, but she didn't say anything or react. I knew it would be hard seeing me with another woman, but she'd have to find a way to deal with that. I wouldn't pull away from my mate to spare her feelings.

Rikki and I ended up being alone in the room as Rachelle took her exit. I turned to walk but Rikki's hand moved to my shoulder, holding me in place. Her hand brushed up my neck and rested at the curve of my jaw, thumb grazing my bottom lip. The touch was enough to send my mind swirling, dazed as if I'd been starved for far too long. I pressed into her hand and felt myself sigh. Eyes closed, I expected to find Rikki's lips on mine but when she hadn't closed the distance, I looked up to find her watching me with a guarded stare.

There was frustration and reluctance in her gaze. Rikki wasn't one to beat around the bush and she certainly wasn't someone who took pleasure in being in second place, but I could see that's how she'd felt now.

"I thought I was doing the right thing."

Rikki nodded. "I know."

I didn't want her to just agree with me. I wanted her to tell me how she felt no matter how much it stung. I'd fucked up staying after learning who Alexis was. And no matter what I'd told myself, I had stayed for my own selfish reasons too. I'd been unsure of how I felt about seeing Rachelle after all these years, but I'd treated our mating bond with little regard.

"I fucked up, Rikki, and I don't expect you to trust me to make the right choice right now, but I'm sorry."

Rikki's teeth gritted and I saw the anger intensify.

"Do you still want her? Because I don't share. For some, it's no big deal. But for me, you are it. I won't sit by and watch you hold her hand and then come back to hold mine."

I wouldn't cry or pretend I didn't know better. I was not innocent, and I left Rikki questioning if I would leave her for Rachelle. All I could do now was make it up to her for the rest of my life.

"I do not want or need her. Not that way."

"What does that mean? Not that way!"

My expression contorted, trying to think of the best way to explain.

"Please don't be angry with me for still loving her but I can promise you, I'm not in love with her. I can also promise that she won't be who I call on when I'm afraid or lonely."

Rikki had been holding me since my legs were still weak, so when I lifted my arm to run my fingers through my hair, she repositioned her hand over my waist.

I rested my hands just above her biceps to keep my balance.

"I want you and only you because you're the one who has my heart. I just know that I also want her to stay in my life if that's even possible because despite how she's been for who knows how long, I know the real Rachelle. You might even like her once she...I don't know. Gets better."

"I can tell something is off with her."

I nodded. "Please be patient with her and trust me a little to know that I mean what I say."

Rikki grunted. "I do trust you."

I sucked in a breath, relieved to hear her say that.

"I won't leave you or the pack again. Not for anyone."

"We face threats together. That's it!"

I nodded. "I still want to find a way to help Rachelle."

Rikki wasn't pleased by that and didn't hide it.

"Isn't that what we do for friends?" I asked.

"She's not trying to be friends," Rikki argued.

"True. But that's all I want from her, and I'll make sure that's clear."

Rikki nodded. This time when she pressed her hand against my cheek she leaned in and captured my lips.

It was all consuming as my breath hitched, needful of more. The kiss was broken before we could go any further and I was unable to stifle my whine.

"Good. It's important to know what you've been missing out on. Don't ever forget it," Rikki whispered in my ear. "But you will shower first before we head home. I do not want to smell that vampire witch on you any more than I have. My wolf can't handle it for much longer. I can't."

When I looked into her eyes, I saw gold and a stern look that left me with no room to argue.

Her dominance made me shiver, my wolf wanting to obey any command she'd give. Rikki rarely used her Alpha magic on me and instead of wanting to argue like I'd done when I first changed, I was downright aroused. She was my mate and my Alpha, and this was a reminder to never forget that.

Chapter Nine

Rikki hadn't been joking about me taking a shower. She waited in the room until I was finished, new clothes in hand. I realized they were mine and put them on tiredly, not energized to lift my arms up over my head, so she helped.

There was still tension between us even though I didn't want to admit to that. It would take time for Rikki to forgive me for staying. She hadn't said she was hurt but her eyes said much more.

I smiled awkwardly, standing beside her and unsure of what to say. She didn't lean in to comfort me, not that I was expecting her to. It was my screw up to fix and I had to trust that we could get through this without any more personal complications.

We made it to the dining hall to find more of Rachelle's servants sitting around the table. There was steak and potatoes, a classic favorite of mine that Rachelle had known would warm my stomach. I moved to an empty chair, not caring who I sat next to and grabbed a fork, digging in. My plate was nearly empty by the time I looked up.

I wiped my mouth with a napkin and smiled cheekily. I scooted the plate away and noticed Rikki sitting next to me with a grin hitching one corner of her face.

"Sorry."

"I have more if you are still hungry," Rachelle offered.

"I'm good for now."

I couldn't help but notice how whoever I'd been sitting next to had shifted far away from me while I'd been too involved with my meal. It appeared that everyone had shifted to the other end of the table, eyes not on me. I took note of Arlana, Susie, the woman I thought was dead but now turned, and the changeling boy but didn't acknowledge them.

Rikki was surely the cause of their behavior though I concluded by Rachelle's soft smile that she'd been the one to orchestrate their repositioning, to avoid Rikki.

"As I was saying before, things are more complicated than you both are aware of. And for that, I know it doesn't seem likely, but they weren't trying to kill you."

"They were trying to take her?" Rikki jumped straight to the question that buzzed on the tip of my tongue.

Rachelle nodded.

"Does this have to do with the vampire Fae that I met with Jaleel?" Things were beginning to make sense.

"Fenix serves under someone who expects you in their court." Rachelle was still being vague.

"They wanted to know if I'd been with you under free will." I studied Rachelle as she nodded again but didn't speak. "Why?" I asked, annoyed.

"Your mother didn't cast you off as a secret to protect you from me, as much as it seems that way." Rachelle seemed offended that others worked hard to make me believe she was the problem. "Your bloodline is bound to me, yes. But not at my doing. We were cursed that way as a form of punishment from the High Priestess. The one before Mira. After my affair with your grandmother, the High Priestess had given me a warning to end things, and I defied her. My feelings for your grandmother were just as important and real to me as my feelings for you."

I would not comment on that, but I just nodded.

Rikki shifted in her chair, leaning her elbow onto the table as she responded.

"How does what happened in the past affect Bonnie now?"

Rachelle's brows raised, dissecting Rikki with a look that told me a small story. She didn't like being talked down to, especially not by a werewolf.

"Please, Rachelle," I begged.

It took her a few seconds to hear my pleading tone.

"It has everything to do with Bonnie now." Her voice came out more like a snarl than the hiss I'd expect out of a vampire. "It was a binding curse that would continue down the Adisa line, always keeping us connected with me craving more than your love… *your blood.* The black witches hoped I'd drain your bloodline until there was no more Adisa."

My eyes widened in shock. "Does Mira know that?"

"Of course, she does. They document everything and it's passed down from one High Priestess to the next. Don't think for one second that she is your ally. The black witches want you dead, they are just not allowed to be the ones to physically cause you harm."

"Why?" I felt like I was going to keep asking that.

"Because they're still bound to you as well. I was your personal ancestor's guardian. And I am still bound to the duty to serve you as guardian. But if I were to have killed you with my blood hunger, that original magic that obligated the witches would dissolve and leave them no longer tied to protect you. Many of the black witches have been killed because of your bloodline."

"Before your grandmother," Rachelle continued, "The Adisa line served under a powerful Fae clan."

It was all starting to make sense. Fenix had offered to take me, but I'd chosen to stay by Jaleel's side and, in extension, to Alexis.

"Over a thousand years ago, it was a blessing for the Adisas to serve the Fae queen. Adisa weren't always werewolves. Adisa was a being of its own within a Fae line."

Her words had shaken me to my core, and I gasped, feeling my body go numb. What did this mean, and what more was I?

"No one knows the kind of Fae your bloodline carried. Not even me, though I have been trying to find out for the past 400 years. Your grandmother thought it best, not that secret." Rachelle watched me but continued. "But when your grandmother came of age, watching the abuse her mother suffered at the hands of the Fae queen, she didn't want to subject her daughters to that same fate. The queen had decided everything for the Adisa lineage. Who they mated with to what sorry soul they had to torture. And if they failed or defied the queen, their punishments were severe. But to the Queen, the Adisas were sworn servants that had no expiration date. All I know is that your Adisa ancestry had once been a tribe of its own until nearly being forced into extinction. They joined the Queen's court for protection."

"Tortured?" I wasn't violent and the thought of performing a hostile act against anyone was unimaginable and made me nauseous.

Rachelle nodded but it was Jaleel who spoke next.

"Adisas were mind manipulators and could make their enemies see the worst things that would make even the strongest person want to kill themselves. Well... are... since you are one."

I snorted. "Does it look like I know how to manipulate someone?"

"You just haven't learned how to tap into that full power, but it makes sense that you are an Omega," Rachelle pointed out. "And why your mother was an Omega."

"But... that's different," I argued. The idea of manipulating someone's mind sounded wrong and dangerous.

"Not really," Rikki added. I gave her a glare but she ignored it. "You could calm our wolves. Prevent them from shifting. That is manipulation. The difference is you do it for the good of the pack."

I never looked at it that way.

"Fuck!" I closed my eyes and nodded. "So, my bloodline is known to be Fae mindfuckers?"

"It was what they were, as you are. Not something they could control being. But they could control who they decided to help or harm. You could do much more than play with someone's mind. You can also help guide them out of possessions and other things."

"Like how I helped that vampire when you possessed him?" I asked.

Rachelle smiled. "I knew you'd help the vampire and wanted to show you that you could."

After one of Amber's vampires had fed from Rachelle's human, Sue, he'd gotten sick. It was only later that Amber noticed the change in Benjamin and requested my assistance.

"You possessed him to test me?" I questioned, finding her methods harsh and unnecessary.

"I did it to help you. It's important you know how to use your gift. You will need it when the worst happens."

Fuck me! Who wanted to hear that the worst would happen? I didn't know what that would look like but her confidence that it would, and the dark distant glare Rachelle held, told me it would be bad.

"Let's fast forward a bit," Rikki said through gritted teeth, containing her emotions a lot better than mine. "Somewhere along the line Bonnie's grandmother mated with a werewolf, had children, and then went to the witches for help. Is that what you're trying to say?"

Rachelle nodded once. "She'd been forced to have children with a werewolf. The Fae Queen wanted to expand the Adisa line and mix with another species."

"To one day…control us?" Rikki asked, vocal cords tightening as she came to that conclusion.

"If she could have the Adisas manipulate multiple packs, she'd be able to have wolves serving as her puppets," Rachelle confirmed.

"The point is, Bonnie is very valuable to the Fae Queen. Not only are you the last of the Adisas, but you are also already connected to a pack and mated to an Alpha. If she has you then she believes she could eventually have your entire pack." Rachelle didn't hold back on the seriousness of my situation.

"But I would never…"

"I know you'd never purposely harm your pack, but the Fae Queen has led this long for a reason. The only reason she couldn't get to you is because your mother hid her pregnancy, and we made it seem like I killed her."

"What?" I snarled.

This time it was Malcolm who spoke angrily.

"You are not innocent. I saw the fear in my mate's eyes directed at you."

"Boy, you are still as naïve as you were the day she died," Rachelle sneered. "It wasn't fear of me but fear, sadness, and her loss of knowing she'd have to sacrifice her life to not be used as a weapon and keep your daughter safe."

"Lies!" Malcolm stood, his chair flying backwards. I watched as his fingertips lengthened into claws anger directed toward Rachelle as if he'd forgotten how powerful she was or just didn't care. "She would have never taken the—"

"What?" Rachelle asked, cutting him off. "Taken the cowardly way out." Rachelle narrowed her eyes, waiting for him to respond. Malcolm just stared defiantly. "Sit your ass down!"

Malcolm had yet to move.

I didn't want to see Malcolm hurt so I whispered calmly, calling on my Omega's gift to speak to his wolf. Reaching out to my Omega gift to sway my father's wolf made me realize just how right Rachelle had been. My intentions were pure, but it was still manipulation.

"I'd die to protect my mate, sister, and every member of the pack," I said. Malcolm blinked as if my words dazed him and turned his head enough to see me. "Not that I'm planning to do that. I prefer to fight. But if I had a child and knew the fate she'd have and could prevent it, I would have probably done the same thing at that time." Rikki reached out and squeezed my hand. "You said it yourself, if she would have trusted in having a pack they could have helped. But you both were alone and faced a Fae Queen. And even now, I'm still making poor decisions because I think if I put space between the people I love, it'll keep them safe."

"But you aren't safe," Malcolm growled.

"No, but I have a better chance because of her sacrifice. Yours. I can't imagine how my life would have turned out if I'd been taken by this queen as a child."

"You didn't know Sonia." Malcolm wouldn't let this go. His love for my mother blinded him from understanding the lengths to which she'd gone to keep me safe. "She would have found another way to keep you safe rather than choosing death."

I'd tried, not for me but for my sister, to keep calm and not snap at the man she adored but he was pushing every button. I didn't know what my mother had even looked like, but I felt compelled to defend the decisions she'd made. Maybe I was like her and that made me feel connected to her in my own way.

"You are right. I didn't get to know her and instead of bitching about her dying without me even knowing what she felt like, I choose to believe she died for me. I hate it, but I can accept it." I couldn't hold back my bitterness, but I could hold back my tears. I wouldn't cry in front of everyone.

"I'm exhausted by lies, secrets, and…" I shut my eyes, tilting my head up at the ceiling and shook it, letting out a groan. "I trust Rachelle. You don't have to like her. No one does. And I wouldn't blame anyone for hating her." I looked to my mate, directing the rest of my words to her, hoping she'd trust in my instincts.

"She's clearly perfect at pretending to be something she's not. A monster." I could feel Rachelle watching me and continued, determined to convince Rikki of what I believed was true. "But she's always had my best interests. In the past and now."

Rikki studied me for a long moment and nodded.

"Okay!" Rikki leaned into the chair, accepting my new reality and what this could mean for the pack. "How do we deal with the Fae Queen?"

Rachelle snorted. "You don't deal with her. Not directly. The only one who can do that is Bonnie." Rachelle tapped her fingernails against the table wryly. "I know it was foolish to believe I could spare you from these truths. Keep you safe. But the truth is…you can continue to hide, or you can let her take you."

"That's what you have to offer us?" Rikki snarled.

I shut my eyes and massaged the corner of my head. It appeared I wouldn't be catching any breaks.

"I can't leave the pack again. I promised not to give in." I looked at Rikki and squeezed her hand. "We do this together."

"That's cute," Rachelle mocked.

Rikki was about to lunge but I reached out and kept a firm grip on her hand.

"We don't have time for this. Don't be an asshole." I wanted to punch Rachelle too, but I didn't have the energy to try. "I won't just hand myself over."

Rachelle smiled. "And that is why I placed you in a corner, terrorizing you and your pack, without killing anyone you cared about. I needed you to feel the loss of separation from your pack and mate so that the next time, when it's real and the Fae Queen is knocking at your door, you fight."

I chuckled. "Oh, so you were teaching me another lesson?" There wasn't enough room in my mind to consider what her words meant without replaying everything since she'd sent Jaleel stalking me.

"Since we're all in agreement that Bonnie won't be giving herself up to the Fae Queen, how do you suppose we handle this? Do you know this queen personally?" Rikki questioned.

"Unfortunately, I do." Rachelle eyes shifted to me tentatively.

I pretended not to notice and kept my gaze angled at Jaleel, who was standing a few feet off to Rachelle's side. If I waited long enough, maybe she'd turn away and focus on something else. The bond between us hadn't dissipated just because I'd decided to leave with my mate. I supposed it would take time to let go of our past and perhaps being away from her would help.

"One last thing before we go." Rikki's anger resurfaced, sensing my emotional struggle to let Rachelle go. "I spoke to the High Priestess. She refused to lift the spell that ties you here."

Rachelle merely shrugged as if being trapped in a cave forever didn't bother her.

"At least you tried."

I narrowed my eyes, doubting Rachelle wasn't angry to hear she'd been denied the opportunity of freedom.

"That's it?" I questioned. "You can't possibly have me believe you're not pissed."

"It doesn't matter what you believe," Rachelle sneered. "You've made your choice."

I growled and huffed out a breath, shifting in my chair. I clenched my jaw shut, fingers digging into my thighs. I wanted to scream and tell her I cared but I knew it would be the wrong thing to do. How was I supposed to care for two different people at the same time, without making one or the other feel unseen?

Every time I felt like I had my emotions in check, one statement would leave me dumbfounded as to how to respond. I knew what I needed and wanted. That Rikki and my pack should be my priority. I also knew I needed and wanted Rachelle in my life. I just didn't know how that would look.

"I advise you to accept help from a mutual friend. If you are going to face the Fae Queen you will need to fight dirty, and we both know that isn't in your nature anymore." Rachelle smiled tightly when Rikki glared at her. "As much as it pains me to see the woman I love move on, it doesn't change my fierce need to see her live for a very long time."

"What mutual friend do you speak of?" Rikki asked through gritted teeth, ignoring Rachelle's taunt.

"Kayla."

That name sounded familiar, and I remembered Rikki and Shiloh mentioning her a few weeks back.

"She's no longer a rogue bounty hunter. She has a pack. A mate and a kid. I won't ask her—"

"It is already done. She will be at your pack by the morning," Rachelle said. "She might be domesticated on the outside, but she'll always be savage and dangerous within. She's not only a werewolf now but a hybrid. And it so happens her maker, Elena, is also mine." Rachelle grinned. "So that makes Kayla my sister. Just be ready to greet her and her sister."

"Sister?" Rikki's brows arched. "It seems I've been out of the loop for a while." Rikki stood. "We should get going."

That was my cue to stand, finding Rachelle beside me before I had a chance to react. Rikki was fast, stepping between us.

"I am not going to hurt her." Rachelle was offended, her eyes never leaving me. "But I would like to speak with you, privately."

I lightly brushed Rikki's arm and found it difficult to speak with Rachelle alone but found the words.

"It will only be a minute." There was something I needed to get off my chest and I couldn't wait.

Rikki sucked in a long breath, her expression indecipherable. If I wanted to play the guessing game, she'd prefer I leave now and never speak to Rachelle again. There'd never been anyone to come between us, but my intuition told me if it were anyone else, Rikki wouldn't have cared. But I chose to sit beside Rachelle when Rikki came for me and chose to stay.

There was a lot I would need to work on if I wanted to keep my mate and keep her loving me. I wasn't perfect and my actions would be a vivid reminder of how wrong I'd been in assuming she'd be fine without me. I'd taken her love for granted.

Rikki left without saying a word but still within view, not trusting that I would come with her or that Rachelle would let me leave. I knew she would not listen in, but I wouldn't whisper and try to hide anything from her. If she asked, I'd tell her whatever Rachelle and I were about to discuss.

"She doesn't look too happy with you." Rachelle couldn't pass up the chance to insinuate my relationship with Rikki had weakened.

"How about you keep your thoughts to yourself when it involves my relationship?" I dug my fingers into my forehead, needing time to relax and not overreact.

This is what Rachelle did when she didn't get her way, pick at something sore and triggering to get my emotions and issues to outshine her own.

"She will never love you the way…"

"Don't!" When I looked at her, my face was constricted with a mix of rage and anxiety, as if being cornered by a bigger predator. I knew my eyes were dark gold. My tongue brushed against my lengthened sharp teeth and shuddered when I bit down, a metallic taste forming in my mouth. I rested both hands at my waist and shook my head. "You are hurting yourself more than me, so stop."

Rachelle averted her eyes and tamped down the vampiric aura she'd been oozing out since Rikki had been here. When she mimicked a breath, I also felt magic dissolve.

"I'm not my grandmother."

Rachelle's eyes widened; her face tight with painful emotion. She stood, her posture straight and unmoving.

I hadn't expected to say that either. But now that it had left my mouth, I realized that's what I'd been feeling under all my struggles regarding our relationship.

"I know you love me but maybe, part of you fell in love with me because of how much I remind you of her. She kept you human, in here." I pressed my fingers against her chest.

Rachelle didn't move. She looked too unnerved to speak, so I continued.

"And maybe I did too. For a while, until you had no choice but to leave me. And I think I understand enough to trust that you genuinely didn't want to leave me. And I no longer hold any anger towards you regarding that." I looked to Rikki, who'd been standing a safe distance away, arms crossed over her chest as she waited.

"I don't know what the future looks like between you and me. But I know enough to know where my heart is now. The thought of leaving here and never seeing you again is unthinkable. But if you want any chance at an honest platonic relationship, you have to accept where my heart is now. I know this all sounds so mundane and like a classic ex-lover speech, but I do know you would rather have me as a friend than nothing. I'm not the same and neither are you. So, can we just try and build something real and honest for the first time? No secrets this time."

The entire time I spoke, Rachelle's expression had changed several times, from a look of defiance and argumentative rage to consideration and possible acceptance. She'd been weighing what mattered most and could see she only had one real option.

There was no chance of staying in my life if she couldn't respect my relationship with Rikki.

"I hear you."

It was the first real sign that Rachelle was truly listening to me.

"And you need to stop playing the 'I don't care who I hurt' game," I said. "Again, it's only hurting you more than me."

Rachelle rolled her eyes, the most human thing she'd done so far.

"Over 400 years of walking this earth, pissing others off makes life less boring."

"That's just childish and sadistic," I said mockingly. "Find a new purpose in life. Pick up a couple hobbies. Help those in need."

Rachelle's face wrinkled, unamused by my suggestions.

I smiled. "You do know what the next step is in showing me I can rely on your word?"

"No, I don't." By her dry tone, she had.

"Release my father."

Rachelle studied me for several of my heartbeats since she no longer had one. I half expected Rachelle to say no but she surprised me.

"One condition."

I nodded.

"When this is all over, you have to come visit me regularly. As friends, of course." She smiled, but added the ending when Rikki shifted, ready to walk back and give her more than a verbal response to her request.

I assumed Rikki had been listening but then I felt a tinge of magic and slapped Rachelle on the arm. She'd been using magic toward Rikki, giving her a sense of concern.

"Fine. It was my last time." Rachelle grimaced. She arched a brow, and I heard Malcolm entering the hall again.

"I was going to come and visit whether it was a condition established or not."

Malcom stood, awaiting Rachelle's order.

"Malcolm, you have serviced my home and shown dire loyalty despite your grievances toward me. And for all who witness see that I, Alexis, sire to many, release you."

Malcolm jolted as if he'd been shaken awake and stumbled backwards until regaining his footing. His shoulders slumped and whatever control Rachelle no longer had over Malcom seemed to deplete him physically.

"He no longer belongs to me so he will be in withdrawal for a few days," Rachelle said. "The stronger a vampire, the stronger those who serve me are. And I am very strong."

I wouldn't question her strength. I was thankful she'd ended up being an ally and not an enemy.

"Thank you," I said.

Malcom didn't bother lingering, perhaps afraid Rachelle would change her mind. I couldn't wait to see Braelin smile when she saw our father.

"I know there's something wrong with you and I have every intention of helping you," I told Rachelle.

"It's not something you can fix."

I smiled, confidence not wavering. "We'll see about that."

Chapter Ten

The drive home was quiet. I would have been lying if I said I wasn't afraid to face my pack. I wondered what they thought of me leaving. Would they still trust me? It wasn't like everyone liked me. I was Rikki's mate and if not for that, I'd be labeled an outsider within the pack.

But what scared me the most was not knowing if Rikki and I would recover from my choices. We were mated through our wolves, but her own heart was a different story. Would we end up in a loveless relationship, only bound together through our wolves? I wouldn't be able to live that way.

The Jeep jerked to a stop, the back door opening as Malcolm stepped out, rushing to Braelin, who stood on the porch in shock. I smiled, happy to see relief loosen her shoulders. When he was nearly to her, she found the ability to move again and leapt off the porch into his arms.

I just watched and found myself tearing up at the sight. My eyes shifted off to my side as Rikki opened my passenger door. I hadn't noticed her exit the vehicle. For whatever reason, I couldn't find a way to move.

"Are you going to hide in here all night?" Rikki's words reminded me of the time I'd been forced to come after learning I'd be turning into a werewolf for the first time. I'd been in complete denial and had sat in the car until Rikki carried me off to her shed.

I stared at the shed now. Our shed. I wouldn't act like a coward hiding inside the car.

"It feels like so much time has passed."

"You haven't been introduced to this world in a positive way. They understand you were only making the best decision you knew to make." Rikki was trying to comfort me with hopeful words.

For a few heartbeats I only stared at Rikki, needing to know if she believed her own words. Maybe she'd spared the pack the truth of who I'd been with and was keeping all the pain to herself.

"I won't lie to them," I finally said.

Rikki's expression blank, she nodded approvingly.

"They all know the truth. There's no reason to lie." There was no affection in her eyes for me. She was guarded and that hurt to see. I'd caused that.

I averted my eyes, ashamed and regretful. When I stepped out of the Jeep, all eyes turned to me. More of the pack had come out of the house, many with expressions I wasn't sure I read correctly. And a few with distrust.

Tato came to me first and embraced me tightly. His strong arms squeezed me, and I felt his genuine happiness in my return.

"I've missed you." His words soothed me, and I couldn't help but cry.

Rosemary came next, giving me a tight hug and shaking me from side to side.

"Don't you ever scare us like that again."

Soon, one by one, more came to embrace me, including Cecelia and her mate and Rikki's second, Toni. It was great seeing everyone. Greenly, Izzy, Ric, and their cub Remy.

Even Lloyd came up with a half grin.

"I look forward to making up for lost time. I had no one to bitch about and I nearly went there to drag you back myself."

I chuckled. "I missed you too." And I did. Lloyd was my pack.

I stood stunned that everyone was happy to see me. I had expected rejection. There were a few that kept their distance but mainly the ones who had never opened up to me.

"I'm sorry everyone. I fucked up, leaving." I had to be honest. The last thing I wanted to do was pretend nothing happened and let it be a sore issue never mentioned.

"It's okay. You are still new to all this," Greenly said, supportively.

"It's no excuse," I admitted.

"And no one's giving you one," Lloyd commented. "You are far from innocent." His brows furrowed but he didn't look angry. "What Greenly was trying to say is, we understand and have all made choices that were very much wrong when starting off in a pack. You are going to fuck up, especially when you carry so much responsibility on those shoulders and you are new to it."

That meant a lot to hear, and I reached out to touch his arm in a show of appreciation.

"Jr will be here by morning," Braelin came and hugged me next. "He couldn't wait until the morning to see you, but I told him to give you the night."

"Thank you." I smiled at everyone. "Thank you."

Everyone nodded and gradually dispersed until I was left with my sister and Malcolm.

I'd noticed Rikki had gone into the shed during my reunion with the pack.

"They all understand and just missed you," Braelin said.

I nodded. "But it's not the same as leaving your mate." I wanted to go hide in a corner and lick my self-pity wounds but couldn't do that.

"She'll forgive you," Braelin whispered.

"You can't promise that." I sighed.

Braelin squeezed my arm. "She loves you. She's angry and no one likes an angry mate, let alone one who's an Alpha, but she loves you." Braelin seemed so confident, and I only wished I had some of her sureness. "Go talk to her."

I nodded. I looked up at Malcolm, who only gave me a reassuring smile, and headed to the shed.

When I opened the front door, I heard the shower running and sighed. I wasn't sure if I should wait or knock on the bathroom door, but I chose the latter.

I moved through our living space to the bathroom around the corner and noticed the door was wide open. Taking a breath, I willed myself to go inside. I took one step and then another, lingering by the door as I turned to the shower, seeing only the shadow of her body through the curtain. My mouth wouldn't move, and I stood frozen, unsure what to do.

I was about to turn around when Rikki whispered out a command.

My heart pounded; eyes wide from her request. No. It wasn't a request. It was an Alpha mate demand.

"Remove your clothes and come into the shower." Rikki's tone was stern, the opposite of suggestive.

This was how Rikki planned to communicate with me, letting her wolf do the leading. I'd do whatever I needed to make my mate happy again, so I began removing my clothes until I stood naked.

Rikki shifted the curtains to let me inside and I did so, as she positioned me in front of her. I let the water splash on top of my head and felt Rikki's breasts brush my back. She held the shampoo bottle in hand and put some in her hand before putting it down. Her fingers combed through my hair, removing the two braids as she washed my hair quietly.

We stood in silence until Rikki was the one who was ready to speak.

Rikki's voice conveyed no emotion. "I've given you too much room to make decisions because you are my mate. But I am Alpha and should have been the one to make the hard choices on how to handle Alexis. You are a newly turned werewolf and it was never your choice to make in sacrificing yourself, let alone staying. I should have commanded you to return. But again, I allowed you to have too much free will because you are my mate." Her fingers cleaned every inch of me. When she turned me to face her, the water ran through my hair, and she worked to remove the soap as her eyes held mine.

"One day you will be a very strong wolf. But that day isn't here yet. You are my mate and an Omega, so that gives you room to make some decisions, but when it comes to the safety of my pack, my decisions need to be the ones that stick. I will always listen to your suggestions and give you space to think of solutions on your own but when it comes to executing those choices, it will be because I approved them and gave the clear. That is how a pack operates. That is why there are Alphas, Betas, and submissives. We all play roles and that is my role. Do you understand that?"

My eyes wide, I nodded quickly. She was right. I was new to this world and instead of learning how to follow, I'd been trying to play leader to a world I was clueless about.

"Shiloh told me what he is and that you knew but he swore you to secrecy, so I'm not upset with you about that," Rikki promised. "I'm only glad to know now because he will be your mentor from here on out until I say otherwise. He will teach you how to use your abilities and whatever else he finds important to share with you. And Tato will continue to train you in combat. And anytime there is an issue that needs an Omega you will continue to do what you have been doing. But nothing more and nothing less."

I nodded, not agreeing just as her mate but under the leadership of my Alpha.

"Do you really understand what I'm telling you?" she asked.

I didn't want to answer without taking the time to think of what she needed me to hear. I'd made the decision to leave without discussing it with her. I tended to question her, not openly but question her nonetheless, on matters that I had no experience in. I brought a human mindset to supernatural issues. If I wanted her to trust me and my decision making, I needed to learn how to shut up and be led.

She wasn't saying forever but until I had time and experience under me.

"Yes, I understand, and I promise I will never leave you again. I promise."

Rikki's brows arched. "And you will never give Alexis any room to try and seduce you again," she snarled.

She'd known what Rachelle tried to several times when I was in the cave. I hadn't planned on keeping that a secret, but her sensing the seductive attempts through our mating bond made me feel worse. I hadn't been able to control Rachelle and her actions, but I should have set my boundaries clearer.

"She knows that there can't be anymore attempts or disrespect of any kind."

Rikki's eyes tightened. "I know what it's like to have loved and lost. And that is the one reason I am trying to be sympathetic to your circumstances with her, but I will not take the insult of you siding with her in any form, ever again. I know she put you in a very uncomfortable position, threatening your sister. Braelin told me what happened while she was there."

Rikki was speaking of me sitting at Rachelle's side when she'd come for me.

"Swear to me, I and this pack will always be first no matter what?" Rikki needed to hear me say the words. Her eyes screamed desperately for me to mean it as her fingers gripped both sides of my arm.

I couldn't stand to see the hurt, anger, and distrust I caused, and promised to myself even if there was a bullet pressed to my head, I'd choose her and my pack every time. "I swear, I'll never allow for anyone, including my own fears, subject me to leaving you and this pack."

"You swear, what?" Rikki's head tilted at an angle, eyes a roaring gold.

My wolf whined, not enjoying our Alpha angry. But there was also a need to be dominated, bitten, fucked, and it was a new feeling I hadn't experienced before. So, when I spoke, I found myself breathless.

"I swear, Alpha."

There was no warning, and I didn't try to move away as Rikki slammed me into the shower wall. I groaned when her teeth scraped across my neck. She growled, body pinning me to the wall and squeezed my breast, tugging on my nipple.

I cried out, head tilting back to give her better access to my neck. I needed to feel her inside me, have her taste me and claim me with her teeth. Too many had tried to claim me for different reasons but the only one I wanted to claim me was her. And I wanted everyone to know. To see that I willingly and proudly wanted Rikki as my mate. It was not just seeing her pain that made me recognize the difference between her and Rachelle, but it was coming home and realizing the loss I could have if she wasn't my mate. How could I show her now that she was my favorite person in the world?

I could be more than my human mind allowed me to be. I could give her more of me.

As she slid her fingers inside me, I whimpered, "Bite me!"

Rikki stopped, keeping her fingers inside as she tilted her head back enough to gaze into my eyes. My clit pulsated and I moved my hand over hers, preventing her from slipping out.

Gold eyes burned into mine, shocked but hopeful. Rikki explained the significance of a mating bite and how substantial it was, but I'd never asked. A mating bite would forever carry the scent of my mate, symbolizing that I was claimed. It would leave no room for someone else to challenge, not unless they were seeking death. I saw it as possessiveness until now. For werewolves, it was a mark worn with pride.

"You don't have to offer me this." Rikki was giving me the chance to back out.

I ran my fingers through her hair and pressed my other hand against hers as her fingers deepened inside me. I moaned, mouth open as I called out to my wolf and my teeth lengthened. I was in so much need, but I wanted to give more than anything. And this was something I could give her. My fangs pierced into Rikki's flesh over her shoulder, and she shuddered. I let her blood fill my mouth and I consumed it, biting down harder.

I winced, body trembling from Rikki's fingernails digging into my flesh. Heat, fierce and all consuming, swirled through me and I let out a gasp. Blood dripped down the corner of mouth, Rikki scooping it with her thumb. I leaned forward, sucking the blood from her finger as she watched with eyelids draped low.

Rikki kissed me again, hungry and wild with need as her fingers began moving inside me. This wasn't soft and timid but rough with a mix of pleasurable pain. The way her fingers felt inside me was indescribable. I equally gave and took, the feel of her skin against mine adding to the friction of pleasure and the build of an orgasm.

I moaned and pivoted my hips, wanting more, tightening around her fingers. I didn't think I could handle anything else but lost all sense of reality when Rikki's fangs pierced my neck. I cried out and trembled uncontrollably and came.

"Ah...fuck!" I cried; face distorted in passion.

Rikki grabbed my jaw, pinning me in place and we locked eyes.

"I am yours and you are mine."

Breathless, body still reacting from my orgasm, I whispered. "I am yours and you are mine." I'd never found those words more powerful than now. Being faced with her pain and anger, I'd make sure I never hurt her like that again. "Always!" I finished.

For the first time since waking up, Rikki's smile reached her eyes.

"I will always love you, Bonnie. I don't say it enough, but I am grateful to have met you. I know it's been hard, and things keep getting in the way, but I promise there will be a day when we won't need to always be in fight mode. That you will see the beauty of being a wolf." Rikki's thumbs grazed my cheekbones, and she kissed my forehead affectionately. "I need you to trust in me. Not just as your mate but as your Alpha. Trust that I will always find you and fight to keep you safe. Trust that this pack would die and kill for you."

I now understood the biggest root of her anger. It was me not trusting in her or the pack. And her own fears that maybe she was not good enough to keep us safe. We weren't under an illusion that she could keep me from being scraped and clawed at but in the end, Rikki would always find me and bring me home if the worst happened.

"Back at you."

Rikki turned the water off, our skin rubbery from being under for too long. She kissed me briefly before moving away. We got out of the shower, dried off and collapsed in bed together.

There was still a way to go but this was a start. I was nearly asleep when we heard a knock at the door.

Instead of my normal disdain at being interrupted, I smiled and knew I'd never complain about the pack disruptions again.

"Alpha," Toni called out from the other side of the door.

"Coming," Rikki grumbled, sliding out of bed. She put on a shirt and shorts and looked at me. "I'll be back."

"Later tonight?" I asked, expecting Rikki to be up all night like she usually did anytime Toni or Tato came knocking.

I flipped the pillow over since it was wet from our damp hair and snuggled under the blanket. I needed sleep and wouldn't be able to wait up for her, but I would try.

"No. I will only be a few minutes. Tonight is about us." Rikki's smile was brief. She opened the door and stepped out, leaving me alone.

I was relieved to know I'd get to lie in her arms tonight. I hadn't checked the time in the last few days, and I didn't care to now. Tonight, I wanted to cherish our relationship and wake up together. Tomorrow I would call my mom and announce my return.

I was nearly asleep when Rikki climbed back into bed. She'd stripped bare and curled into my body, arm draped across my waist. I blinked slowly, fighting my sleep and grazed the tip of my finger over the bite on her shoulder.

"It's still here," I whispered lazily.

Rikki's face rested against my shoulder, and she yawned. Rikki was never tired, and it surprised me.

"And it will stay. We called to our wolves to share a mating bite. It will heal but the mark will never go away."

"I'm too tired to try to understand." Magic was a confusing thing. My eyes widened, realizing something. "You bit me on the neck," I said.

Rikki nodded. "And just big enough for Alexis or anyone else to never forget it."

I snorted and accepted Rikki's choice of where to place the bite.

"Fair enough. You deserved to put it wherever you wanted."

"And if I wanted to place it between your thighs? Then what?" Rikki's voice was lustful and husky.

I smiled, my nipples tightening from the possibility of her mouth being between my legs. We were both tired, but a few days of separation made our need to make love outweigh sleep.

"Then I'd have to find a new spot of my own to nibble at."

"You are thinking about my ass, aren't you?" Rikki lifted her head, scrutinizing me briefly before laying back down.

I *was* thinking about her ass. It was perfectly round and firm as if she did lunges daily. I licked my lips, fingers eager to squeeze her ass if I could reach it.

"You brought it up first."

"I did and as much as I would like to feel your hands squeeze me, you need to sleep," Rikki whispered. "And I'm saying that as your Alpha. We have a long day ahead of us and you're still recovering."

With that, any attempt to seduce Rikki extinguished. I would take the words she said to me in the shower seriously and listen to my Alpha when commanded.

"Yes, Alpha," I responded, fatigue easily causing my eyelids to feel heavy again.

It didn't take long for my eyes to close completely and let the night be the only other thing to claim me.

Chapter Eleven

"Bonnie, get your ass up!" There was a loud bang on the door, and I jolted, startled by the invasive sound. I'd nearly shoved Rikki off the bed, thinking I was back in the cave with a chain wrapped around my neck. I'd been dreaming and being awoken from screaming through the door wasn't a great way to wake up.

"I'm going to kill your friend!" Rikki grumbled through gritted teeth, shifting to sit up in bed.

"Not if I do it first," I agreed. I tossed the covers off me and groaned when Jr called out again.

"Jr. Give us a damn minute please." I loved him and understood his eagerness to see me, but Goddess help me, I wanted to strangle him right now.

I heard Jr move away from the door, probably realizing two angry wolves would come out due to his early morning wakeup call. I looked at the window where the curtain was cracked enough to see outside and noticed only a tinge of dark orange and red in the sky.

Rikki grabbed her phone and snarled.

"It's barely six."

Dressed, I headed to the door and grumbled my disdain. When I opened it, Jr forgot the word 'boundary' and reached to pull me into a tight embrace that would suffocate a mundane woman. Fortunately for me, I was all werewolf with fangs to show for it.

"Jr, out," Rikki demanded. She was still naked underneath the blankets.

He let me go and I shoved him out of our home, closing the door behind me. I wanted to punch him, but I'd missed him too, so my annoyance vanished. I reopened the door, and he reached in again; this time I sank into his grip and told him I missed him. He was still recovering from his injuries but looked far better than how I left him.

"You fucking scared the shit out of me." He stood bent to one side, probably aching from squeezing me too hard.

"I know. Trust me, it wasn't my intention."

Braelin stepped onto the porch, brows kneaded in a deep frown.

"I told you to wait until morning!" she chastised.

Jr pointed to the dark orange painted sky.

"It is morning."

"And you shouldn't be on your feet!" she countered.

That made Jr smile.

"Why? Do you care?" he asked, snarky.

Clearly, nothing had changed between them. Braelin refused to entertain Jr with an answer and turned away.

"It doesn't look like you've made any progress in wiggling your way into her heart." I watched Jr stare at the now empty porch, stuck in a daydream.

"Jr…" I waved my hand over his face, trying to get his attention.

"Yeah…" Jr smiled as if he'd heard Braelin calling his name. He turned to me with a serious expression. "She will be my mate. She's just in denial but I'm patient."

I stared at him for a long time, amazed by his confidence. This was more than a crush or infatuation for Jr, and I knew I had only one choice to make. Support him.

"She's had a tough life and has been on her own for half of it. Maybe tone down the silly humor and show her the side of you I know she needs to see."

"What side exactly?" Jr asked, genuinely wanting to know.

I patted his shoulder. "The side that's sweet. Knows how to listen. Loyal and protective. Has the ability to hold her when she cries and never judges, because that's the side she needs. She also needs your smile and humor, but she just doesn't know it yet."

Rikki chose this moment to come out. Her eyes narrowed on Jr in warning while extending her arm to me. I slid along her side, curling into her and pressed my nose into her neck. That wild rosemary scent I loved enveloped me.

"Do you like annoying me?" Rikki asked.

I assumed the question was directed at Jr and turned to face him, smiling awkwardly.

"Uh…not on purpose." Rikki's brow raised and he cleared his throat. "I mean no." His eyes averted to the ground. "Alpha," he added.

If I didn't know any better, Jr was treating her like she was his Alpha and not as if he were a human outside of our pack. I knew he'd wanted to be turned but again he surprised me with his serious expression.

Rikki and I both looked at each other briefly and she nodded.

"Then don't bang on our door like that ever again, especially this early."

"Yes, Alpha." Jr lifted his head long enough to glance my way. Expression wry, he was trying to gage how I felt about his demeanor toward my mate and convey that I had no room to talk him out of it.

I wanted Jr to be happy and he was a grown man. He joked a lot, but he knew when something was too important to overlook. Wanting to be changed wasn't anything to overlook so I nodded, showing my support. In the end, it would be only Rikki's decision to change him, and I wouldn't try and influence her decisions. She was Alpha and bringing a new werewolf into the world was a big responsibility I knew nothing about.

The lights in the main house turned on and I knew more of the pack was waking up from Jr's unexpected wake up call.

We walked into the house. The kitchen was filled with fresh baked goods: donuts, croissants and other delicious pastries.

"At least I brought breakfast. I also had to go to IHOP to get a whole lot of bacon and sausage. You can imagine what they thought when they took my order." Jr stepped into the kitchen, putting on an apron that had been tucked away in one of the cabinets.

He was limping and moved as if he ached but that didn't seem to slow him down. Jr was acting like a cadet in the fire department, working to make a great and lasting impression. I assumed Rikki was the chief in his eyes.

Rikki tilted her head to whisper in my ear.

"He's been doing stuff like this since you left."

I was impressed. One by one, those who lived in the main house or had stayed the night filled the kitchen, taking turns gathering the food they wanted and heading to the main dining hall. Clearly everyone was comfortable with Jr, and I hoped he got what he wanted because it seemed he was already fitting in well with the pack.

I expected to see Raine come down and glanced toward the stairs, waiting. She was the pregnant human I'd found in the illegal clinic the night Tato and I went off to find evidence of where Rikki had been taken. She'd been tied down, scared and alone and it had taken time for her to accept the new life she would have to lead as a mother to a werewolf cub.

"She's not here." Rikki sensed who I was looking for and explained. "After you…left with the reptilian vympyrus, Shiloh did exactly what you asked. He told me he was an Omega and that he'd take care of Raine like you requested."

I could hear her struggle in mentioning my choice to leave with Jaleel. I was under no illusions that it would take time and the right kind of choices on my end before Rikki could move on completely. I wouldn't defend or make excuses for my actions.

"But why did she leave?" I asked.

Rikki's shoulders stiffened. Her expression was volatile as she tried to explain.

"Perhaps, it's because we don't have a relationship and he's been lying to me all these years. He thought it was best she came with him verses him staying here."

I heard the hurt in her voice. I wanted to be gentle with my words, but she needed to hear the truth too.

"He lied, but it also means the choices he made years ago weren't done out of malice. Maybe, he was just lonely and wanted to have a sister."

"He should have told me the truth," she hissed.

If the pack was listening, they pretended otherwise.

"You expected him to tell his sister, who denied him. Granted he made the wrong choices." I knew what that felt like. Being an Omega didn't mean I was immune from poor decision making. "But you wanted him to share his deepest secret. A secret that during that time, might I add, was big enough to get him killed." A secret I couldn't bear having even now.

I hadn't said that last part aloud, but Rikki could sense what I'd been thinking.

She huffed.

"Alpha." Rosemary walked up with a plate of food for both of us. She grinned at me as we took the food offered.

We walked to the table crowded with werewolves and found a seat next to my sister and Nelia, a submissive wolf who'd I'd fought beside when our pack was attacked here by a man who'd thought he had a right to claim me. She was sweet and polite, but I'd heard her when she didn't think I was listening. Her mouth was as foul as Lloyd's.

We smiled and she bumped her shoulder against me playfully.

"Can you call Shiloh and ask him to bring her? I need to see her for myself." I didn't know where my phone was and hadn't thought to check. This was the longest I'd been without one and it felt freeing.

"He's already been called," Tato explained, tearing a piece of bacon off with his teeth. "Along with other pack members. We have a pack meeting in one hour."

I nodded. There was a lot to cover since my unexpected departure. I tossed a small piece of bacon in my mouth, feeling self-conscious and chose to stare at the plate. There were a few that were looking at me accusingly. It wasn't hard to guess that I would be the focus point of the meeting.

"We should call your mother first and let her know you're back," Rikki said. "But if we want to keep her safe, it's best she stays home until this over."

I nodded my agreement to Rikki and sighed. Braelin gave me a knowing smile and looked at our father, who had been sitting quietly.

His eyes shifted from Braelin to me at the mention of my mother slash sister. Gosh, this was all so weird. I don't know how I was supposed to keep this all from her. Could I? I thought I would but after leaving and what happened, there was no real explanation of what had happened the day I left. They'd kept my mom from seeing me stabbed and carried off, but she knew that Rikki hadn't told her the real story.

I hadn't expected to blurt out the words.

"She needs to know." I looked at my sister and Malcolm and then Rikki.

"I know." Rikki nodded. "She's called everyday asking if I found you. She's no fool."

I nodded. "Besides, my brother knows the truth. If we keep this from her, there will always be a distance between us. She'll miss out on my life. Braelin's life. Our father's." I looked at Malcolm. "And I just can't lie to her anymore." It was one of the main reasons I kept pushing her away.

I could see the possibility of creating a real relationship with my mother dancing in both Braelin's and Malcolm's eyes. They'd wanted her to know but wanted it to be up to me to tell her. I wouldn't be selfish in keeping her all to myself. I knew it wouldn't be easy and she'd have a whole lot of angry words before she listened, but she was reasonable, and I trusted she could handle the truth.

"I want to thank you for opening your home to me," Malcom said. "I don't expect anything out of this and can figure things out on my—"

Rikki raised her hand and Malcolm fell silent. "I'm not about to kick you out. This pack needs more members. Strong ones. Loyal ones. So, if you can follow my lead, then all we need is a ceremony during the full moon."

That made Braelin smile, eyes tearing in relief.

It didn't take Shiloh long to arrive, every member of the pack sitting out in the backyard. Shiloh walked in and I tried to hide my surprise, observing his proximity to Raine, close enough that their shoulders brushed together every time one moved.

Raine rested a hand over her swollen belly, no discomfort or pain showing as Shiloh held her other hand and guided her to an outdoor sofa on the patio. We'd moved the table off to the side and Rikki stood on top, glancing down at most of the pack sitting on the grass and on lawn chairs. I stood off to the side, leaning against the wall next to the sliding door. Since the focus would be on me, Rikki thought it best that I stand atop the patio deck as if enough attention wasn't already on me.

Rikki gave her brother a half nod, no sign of inner rage or annoyance toward him. I thought that was progress. I waved to Raine once she was seated and she smiled, waving back. Rikki ordered Jr to go home, pack business being only pack business.

The pack whispered guesses at what Rikki was about to share.

"What did Bonnie do now?" I heard one of my pack members ask.

"Probably pissed someone off by opening her big mouth," someone snickered.

I hated hearing how some of my pack felt about me, but it was something I could either whine about or ignore. I hadn't won any extra friends by leaving them and ultimately insinuating that they weren't strong enough to keep me and my brother safe. It wasn't how I felt but they didn't know that and trying to make excuses wouldn't do me any service.

It was Greenly that silenced them.

"I'm sorry but was it you who couldn't beat her in a fight when our Alpha was taken, and you tried to take advantage of the situation? How about the fact that she held this pack together after being in the pack for just a few months?"

By their lack of response, I figured they had nothing else to say. Greenly looked up at me and winked.

I was also thankful it wasn't Rikki defending me. Many didn't feel comfortable speaking their mind about me, afraid Rikki would react harshly, and I had asked her a while back to leave them alone. We had to work through this, and I had to be the one to face them. I wouldn't win everyone over, but I didn't care. There were a few assholes in the pack. I considered them distant relatives I never wanted to see.

"I want to thank everyone for showing up and on time." Rikki's voice silenced everyone.

I moved to the steps on the patio and sat at the top. So far, all eyes were on Rikki, awaiting the big news.

"Five minutes from now we will have a visitor. An old acquaintance who has a nation-wide reputation as a rogue bounty hunter." Rikki was doing a great job at hyping this woman up.

"Are you talking about Kayla?" Ric asked. He looked star struck, a gleeful smile brightening his eyes.

Whispers swarmed through the pack until Rikki spoke.

"Yes. She'll be here with her sister, Rachel. There's a lot to discuss, so please keep your comments to a minimum. Time isn't on our side."

We heard movement in the house, footsteps approaching a few seconds later. Toni opened the sliding door and stepped through, two women behind her at a distance.

I twisted to get a good look at the older woman about my age walking out first. She had brunette chin-length hair and striking green eyes. She was a perfect example of what a stem in a leather jacket and loose jeans looked like.

The younger woman, possibly in her early twenties, had a certain swag about herself too but was a little more casually dressed, like a college student in a rush to get to class. She had on designer maroon sweatpants with a white shirt that had an image of two ducks going at it.

It wasn't an outfit I expected anyone to wear to a werewolf meeting, let alone to meet people for the first time.

Rikki greeted both women and stepped closer to me, giving them room to stand closer to the center.

"It's been a long time." Rikki's diplomatic and professional approach showed in the way she held the gaze of both women before bowing and waving to the pack. "We are very appreciative that you drove all this way to assist us."

The woman I assumed was Kayla bowed her head back.

"It feels good to be amongst another female Alpha. My sister, Rachel."

Rachel nodded but didn't move to offer a hand.

Rikki turned and extended her hand out to me. I took it and stood to face both women.

"My mate and our pack Omega, Bonnie."

"That's freaking dope." Rachel moved closer and sniffed me.

I tried not to look uncomfortable but failed, both my brows raising.

"Rachel," Kayla grumbled under her breath. "An Omega isn't tracked through smell, and you know that."

Rachel smiled apologetically. "Sorry."

"Please forgive my sister's behavior," Kayla said. "She's inexperienced and this is her first time out of our pack's territory. She spoiled and thinks it's appropriate to sniff others, apparently."

Rachel rolled her eyes but said nothing.

"It's nice to meet you both. Not the best of circumstances but I'm learning that's the way of life as a werewolf." I shook Kayla's hand and smiled when I noticed Rachel reach in to formally greet me as well.

Rikki took the opportunity to introduce her pack to Kayla and a few other significant members before getting to the purpose of why they were here.

"I'll get straight to the point." Rikki faced the pack. She hadn't informed anyone of what we'd learned, and I was sure to get more pack members wishing for my disappearance after everything was shared.

"I'm going to admit, I'm inexperienced fighting Faes. I'm not sure how much Alexis has shared with you." Rikki paused and waited for Kayla to confirm what she knew.

Kayla nodded. "Alexis has shared everything."

Rikki nodded and informed the pack of everything.

Plenty of stares were aimed my way. That was no surprise, and I chose to ignore them.

"I won't lie to you. The Fae Queen is as evil as it gets," Kayla sneered as if she had personal history with the Fae Queen. "I don't know her personally, but I know of her through another Alpha in Yosemite. This Fae Queen fights dirty and kills messy. And she has no problem using her own hands though she prefers not to. You would have to piss the Queen off to get her out of the castle."

"Castle?" I frowned. "Do you mean metaphorically?"

"No." Kayla grinned. "You can only reach her castle through a portal."

If I hadn't gone through a portal with Jaleel recently, I would have doubted its existence, but another realm was a far stretch from jumping to a new location. The energy in the pack shifted, tasting Rikki's frustration about the difficulty to reaching the Fae Queen first before she came banging on our door. We were at a disadvantage, exposed, and had the potential to face a violent attack at any moment.

"That doesn't leave us with many options." Tato stated the obvious, ignoring my wide-eyed stare. "We can't just wait for the Faes to show up."

"No," Kayla agreed. "You have to lure her out. Or at least someone who represents her court."

"Fenix." I hadn't intended to blurt that out. "They gave me the impression that they held high rank in the Fae's court."

Kayla shook her head. "They're not someone you can or want to catch. They're also vampire. Slick fucker."

Being reminded of Fenix as a vampire Fae hybrid, I tried not to stare at Kayla's mouth, expecting fangs to protrude. I smiled tightly and looked away.

"Are you suggesting we lure and capture one of the Queen's court Faes?" Rikki had been able to read between the lines.

"She only cares about her court Faes. Take one of them…she'll send out a bigger fish and that is where you play a game." Kayla explained the trickery of Faes and using the right words to create an outcome aimed toward what we wanted.

"I'm confused. Are you saying we have to blackmail her into leaving Bonnie alone? And how do we know she'll keep her promise?" Toni didn't trust the advice, arms crossed over chest in doubt.

"Yes." Kayla nodded, leaving no confusion.

"We don't do that," Rikki disagreed.

"Then why am I here?" Kayla asked. "Alexis said you'd do anything for your mate, or was she speaking more for herself?" Kayla tone wasn't harsh or threatening and she wasn't trying to start an argument.

I could tell my mate hadn't liked being questioned and it took her a minute to read what Kayla was trying to do. If Rikki wasn't committed to making tough decisions, she would have refused Kayla's offer to help. It seemed Rachelle had known my mate's tolerance to violence more than I expected.

"The thing about Faes, they love bargaining, and they cannot lie. But they are very sneaky and know how to find loopholes." Kayla continued, figuring if Rikki wasn't willing to listen, she'd have been refused by now. "Faes are just as good at manipulation and tricking you into agreeing with them like vampires, all without enthralling you. They use words that appeal to your nature and twist them for their own personal gain. Capturing a Fae will tip things in your favor and leave you with options."

"What would we bargain with?" Rikki questioned.

"What are you willing to sacrifice?" Kayla asked.

"I have nothing—"

"Not you," Kayla said, cutting Rikki off. "You?" Her eyes were on me.

I shook my head, dubiously. "I don't have anything. I know you don't mean materialistic things, so I don't know what she'd want."

"She wants you and your gifts. Usually, Faes like to stay to themselves but she likes some Faes to breed with other supernaturals, whether it's through birth or through a bite." Kayla was sharing a lot I would have to think about. "You are every bit a wolf as you are of a Fae line. I will teach you words to use, avoid, and ultimately how to tip the scales in your favor. But this won't matter if we don't catch a court Fae."

"And how do you suggest we do that?" Toni asked, no longer expressing doubt.

"Set a trap," Kayla said. "Alexis knows a Fae who serves the Queen. He won't be easy to grab, but I know where he'll be tonight. All I need to hear is a yes."

Rikki looked at me, searching for the right decision. I'd heard her words last night and wouldn't try to throw my opinion out there if I wasn't the one risking the pack's integrity. She would be crossing a well-maintained line.

The pack watched our Alpha, awaiting her decision.

Toni stepped forward before Rikki could speak.

"If I may, Alpha?" Toni was always hard for me to read. He stayed professional with me all the time and never broke free from overindulgent politeness.

"Speak your mind," Rikki encouraged.

Toni addressed the pack. "I will be honest. Since Bonnie's joined the pack, life has not been boring."

I masked my shock and smiled tightly, not expecting Toni to remind the pack of their troubles because of me. It wasn't as if I'd searched for trouble and had been bitten for it. My life was thrusted into the supernatural world, and I merely landed on their doorstep. Before I could dose myself with self-pity and a grain of salty emotions, Toni continued.

"She's inexperienced, stubborn, and doesn't know when to sit still." Toni wasn't holding back on pointing out my flaws. "But she's not just our Alpha's mate but also our pack member. For better or worse."

"You have point to make?" Rikki asked, keeping her eyes on him. She hadn't liked what he had said so far but stood patiently.

"We use her when we need a pack member to regain control, or when someone's hurt. Or to help our mates reach a full-term pregnancy, and not once has she asked for anything in return. She didn't ask for this life either, but most of us did. And yet, we judge her. But I know if my mate needed me and my only option was to tear through every threat in order to keep her safe, I wouldn't blink. Our Alpha needs our support. Bonnie needs our support. We don't have to be cruel in our hearts. But we can surely act that way when it comes to keeping our own safe."

Toni and Rikki shared a moment, no words spoken but a lot said. The message was understood. If our pack was going to survive, it meant changing how others viewed us. We could be loyal to our allies, fair, and sympathetic to those in need but to anyone who wanted to see us as enemies, we needed to change. Perhaps killers. Perhaps not. But something harsher.

"I haven't experienced a pack of rogues or an attempt to destroy or control my pack in over two years. Unfortunately for my enemies, my reputation is unforgotten. What reputation do you and your pack want to create?" Kayla had a lot of experience to offer, and I found myself curious about her story.

For a while, no one spoke. The pack snuck peeks at one another, deciding what was right and wrong. The suggestion of change was a decision that everyone had to make, because that meant the pack as a whole would have to take on the responsibility that accompanied it.

"I'm tired of being looked down on as just a submissive." Nelia stood taller than I'd ever seen. She was mixed with black and Korean, turned during World War Two. Her father had migrated to America and met her mother. Both were killed during the war, leaving Nelia alone and newly turned. She'd told me how a pack of wolves took her in and lived on the streets to avoid the war. Werewolves couldn't handle too much blood without losing control unless they were much older.

Whatever courage she had, I'd always known it was there from just learning her story.

Nelia looked to our Alpha, not dropping her gaze until Rikki looked back. When she had, Nelia averted her eyes and continued. It wasn't defiance on Nelia's mind but rather wanting to make sure she was heard.

"If we don't learn how to be stronger, faster, and tougher, we won't last much longer. But more than that, we need to learn how to be a pack that isn't together just to feel safe. We need unity. I choose this pack and that means I choose every single one of you. For better or worse."

"We need to respect each other." Greenly spoke up, avoiding standing. "Respect our dreams, passions, who we love. And see each of us as capable wolves in order to keep this pack safe."

I was amazed by the pack's reaction and the potential we had. I didn't want to ruin the moment by speaking and continued to watch.

"I certainly look forward to the change. Seems to me, we are up for one." Tato began flipping a throwing knife up and down and catching it without the sharp end ever digging into his palm. "So, are we going to catch a Fae or not?"

Tato's question was directed at Rikki. Everyone was quiet as we watched her contemplate. When Rikki's eyes shifted to mine, I knew she'd made up her mind.

I guess we were going to catch a Fae.

Chapter Twelve

After creating a plan and going over it several times, we were packed into Rikki's Jeep, headed to Portland. All the major players liked to be in Portland, finding innocent humans to feed on and manipulate. I sat in the passenger seat but twisted around, leg curled under me, to face Kayla seated in the back.

Ric, Cecelia, Tato, and Braelin were in the second vehicle following close behind. Rikki wanted Toni to stay with the pack and act as Alpha in case something went wrong. It was a formality Rikki practiced every time she left on a dangerous task. Shiloh promised he would meet us there, wanting to gather more intel of his own first.

Rachel sat beside her older sister, listening proudly as Kayla shared stories after I'd asked about her life as a bounty hunter.

"What made you go back to your pack?" I asked.

There was an awkward silence. Kayla attempted a smile but gave up, her expression impassive.

"Sorry. That question was invasive." I turned to face the front, giving Rikki a timid smile. She reached out and squeezed my thigh.

"My father was murdered." Kayla's tone was calm, but I heard the tension. "Our father," she corrected. I kept my mouth shut and listened. "But what you meant to ask was why I left the pack in the first place."

Rachel spoke for her sister, and I could hear the love and care in her voice.

"Our father made the biggest regret of his life. He disowned her for loving another woman."

"I never knew that," Rikki said.

Kayla grunted. "How could you? I lived in my wolf more times than I could count when we first met and never shared my history."

"And when our dad was murdered by our piece of shit uncle, Kayla returned and, long story short, became Alpha," Rachel finished.

I turned and found Kayla sitting with an upsetting expression as if that wasn't the whole story.

"And that woman you loved?" I asked.

Kayla smiled. "She is my mate. Her name's Nina."

"Now that's an ending worth living for," I chuckled.

"Agreed." Kayla tilted her head toward the window. It was early afternoon and night wouldn't come for hours. "In case you're wondering, the sun doesn't bother me at all. I was turned almost two years ago. Not by choice, but nor was it my maker's."

"Maker?" I wasn't aware of vampire terminology and wanted to educate myself more on vampires and other supernatural.

"Yes. Some vampires call their makers sire, but I don't serve under my maker. A sire is just a name that is used when a vampire serves their makers," Kayla explained. "I am both vampire and werewolf, but I can still shift into my wolf's skin. I also have vampire fangs and need to drink blood from time to time."

My brows arched, taking in the hybrid lessons given, and let out a breath.

"You might not see it now, but you are a hybrid. There is a quarter Fae in your blood and soon you'll figure out what that means for you," she said.

I turned back just as we were exiting the highway. I had to admit, I was relieved since I didn't know how to face that reality. I hadn't taken in the fact that I had Fae blood in me until now.

"We should be there in a few minutes," Rikki announced.

The rest of the car ride went in silence. Rikki parked along the main street, a block from where we needed to go. Whereas werewolves and vampires tended to cause trouble at night, Faes were daylight beings.

I was beginning to understand there were a variety of Fae beings. Maerel came to mind as I could now separate how they were different, not in just how they looked but in their abilities. Maerel was the Fae changeling I had met when Rikki was taken, ultimately helping me find my mate. Then I remembered the water Fae who I now knew served Rachelle. Meeting the water Fae wasn't a fun experience since it tried drowning me by forcing water into my lungs, while standing by the river. And then there was Fenix. They'd given me the impression of being stronger and deadlier than both Maerel and the water Fae combined. Fenix was both vampire and Fae and I knew there had to be a big story behind that.

But what was I? What kind of fae? I was sure only the Fae Queen knew the answer. I still didn't know what I could bargain with the Queen, but I needed to figure it out soon.

Everyone was out of the car when I finally looked up except Rikki, who'd been watching me. My life had just been starting to make sense and then Rachelle reentered my life, along with Faes. There was a lot I needed to say to Rikki but found my mouth locked in place.

She reached out, fingers grazing my cheek. "I know."

That was all she said, and I wanted to ask what she knew. I didn't even know what I had been trying to say.

"Bonnie. Not everything has to make sense right away. You don't need all the answers and no matter what, you won't lose me." Rikki said all the right things and that was what I what I needed for now. I needed her confidence that we would make it through everything.

"I love you!"

Rikki grinned. "I love you too."

We got out of the car and found everyone gathered in a huddle as if we were on a team going over a play. I smiled as they made room for us to huddle in.

"As I said before, Faes don't give out their names. Knowing a Fae's name is like holding a piece of their power. That's why we call the Fae Queen, queen."

"But what about the Fae I met?" I asked.

Kayla nodded. They're more than Fae. Only mixed blood Faes and lesser Faes can give out their names without consequence to them. But even then, Fenix could not be their real name."

That made sense.

"We can call this Fae Smauggler," Kayla said, her face blank. She didn't smile, and I wondered if she ever did. My gut told me she only smiled for the people she loved. "People actually call him Smaug."

"What's so special about Smaug's restaurant?" Ric asked, confused to why a Fae would own one.

Kayla had waited to share more about Smaug until now.

"His restaurant is a Fae playground. One of the few outlets Faes have in the human world. It is not something you'll miss when you walk in. The music can be hypnotic so don't go dancing in the circle you see in the middle of the restaurant."

"Why?" I asked. I felt like I'd heard fairytale stories about Fae's growing up and what Kayla was telling us sounded familiar. Maybe not everything in the mythology section in libraries or on TV was made up.

"Because you'll end up dancing for centuries before you have a chance to snap out of it," Shiloh answered, appearing through a mist that still lingered behind us.

Kayla nodded her head in agreement. "We go in like curious wolves, because the Faes will know what we are the moment we enter. But don't eat or drink anything. Do not thank them or ask for anything."

"Won't that draw suspicion on us if we just go in and sit?" Tato asked, incredulously.

"No," Rikki answered. "Because we will be there with Bonnie, a newly discovered Fae. They will know what she is, right?" Rikki asked Kayla for clarification.

Kayla nodded once. "Even a drop of Fae in you is all they need but you aren't of a weak Fae line. Having a quarter Fae is just as significant as being full Fae in their eyes."

"But how do we really know I'm of a strong Fae line? I don't know what kind of Fae I am." I tried not to sound bitter about that, but I knew it came out in the way I held my jaw closed.

"The Fae Queen would never have a lesser Fae serve right under her, let alone work so hard to get you back," Kayla pointed out.

That made sense.

"Smaug will want to sway you to join him for a drink. In his eyes, if he convinced you to return to the castle, the Queen would grant him anything his heart desires." Kayla seemed so sure of everything, and I couldn't help but believe in her plan. "Opportunities for power don't come often for Faes, so he won't miss the chance."

"And because I'm quarter Fae, I can eat or drink the food," I asked.

Kayla nodded. "Remember, Faes can't lie but they can twist the truth. You might be able to since you aren't full Fae, but I bet even you struggle to lie and it's not just because of your human moralistic values. Lying actually sickens a Fae."

I nodded. I could do this. All I needed to do was play as if I was interested in the part of myself that was new to me and wanted answers. I could ask questions and eventually get him to a space that led away from other Fae eyes just in time for Rikki and the others to grab him. And part of me was interested. It was the same as discovering I was adopted by my sister and wanting to know who my birth parents were. Now, I wanted to know the other part of me that wasn't merely werewolf but something more.

"We'll go in only as support," Braelin said.

She and Ric would be the only ones to enter the restaurant. Too many werewolves would make Smaug nervous. Rikki and the others would hide and find a way in.

As if reading my mind, Shiloh said, "I know a way in. I have a Fae of my own who will slip us through the back at the right moment."

I could see surprise followed by pride reach through Rikki's eyes, aimed at her brother. There was a future for them yet. I smiled.

"Ready?" My sister asked.

I nodded. “Let’s get this over with.” I was nervous and wouldn’t pretend. It would be realistic coming into a Fae establishment nervous since I was going into enemy territory.

Before I could face this new challenge, I needed to absorb some of Rikki’s confidence. I leaned in to kiss her on the mouth.

Rikki smiled into my kiss, brushing her fingers through my hair.

“I got you,” she whispered, and I believed her, kissing her deeper before pulling away.

I turned and walked the block toward the restaurant with my sister and Ric at my side.

*

From the outside of the restaurant, I would have never guessed it was owned by a Fae and a trap for humans. The structure was folksy, unassuming, and modest, giving the illusion of safety. Stacked stones made up the outer structure of the restaurant and it was hard to see through the darkened windows, but there was a warm noise that could be felt. The sound of violin and folk style music had such a melodic rhythm, it was almost tempting to sway. I took that to be the hypnotic tune Kayla had warned us about.

As I opened the heavy, wooden door, I could smell baked pies and other sweets that could easily melt in my mouth and groaned. The restaurant was packed with people gathered around long booths, while others were occupied at smaller tables, looking as if they were reaching their drinking limit. They were singing loudly, while I noticed people at the center of the restaurant were dancing carelessly, drinks in hand. Their eyes looked hollow as if they were blacked-out drunk but couldn't stop moving.

No one seemed to mind, unaware of what was happening to them. It wasn't too bright, a dim chandelier bringing most of the light into the space.

Several eyes darted our way, curious and inquisitively, waiting to see where I would go. If they were looking at me that meant they were Faes and were aware of what I was.

A man with bright green eyes and elegant features approached with a smile that would seduce any number of humans. He was very handsome but so were all the other Faes I'd noticed.

"Please. Take a seat anywhere. You and …" He eyed Braelin and Ric briefly, giving nothing away as he finished. Your friends."

I nodded and was about to say thank you but stopped myself.

He noticed me open my mouth before shutting it and grinned.

"You are Fae as well. Saying thank you will bring you no inconvenience."

He knew why I hesitated. I nodded and decided I wouldn't take any risks and walked toward an open booth. Fae eyes followed me, and I pretended not to notice. Braelin sat beside me while Ric sat across from us.

"This place is…jolly!" Braelin glanced around cautiously.

"Yeah," Ric grumbled. "I feel bad for the many souls who've been manipulated here."

"You think that was Smaug?" I asked. It wasn't like we had a picture of the Fae.

Braelin scrutinized our surroundings, watchful of the Faes closest to us.

"Not likely," she whispered.

The Fae who had invited us to sit was no longer in sight, probably telling the owner of the establishment I was here.

I let out a shaky breath. "This is weird."

Braelin squeezed my hand, understanding what I meant. Not too long ago, I'd been living a human life until I was attacked, and my wolf was forced out. I then found out my mother was my sister, and I had a whole set of biological parents out in the world. Reuniting with Rachelle had been another major surprise. Now I was part Fae with a Fae Queen expecting my loyalty to her court.

"The only thing I can hope for is there being a purpose to all of it." Braelin looked off to the side and noticed the Fae who let us in. Alongside him stood a shorter man with the same green eyes but with a wide brawny build. His ears, along with all other Faes', were pointy at the tips and faced outward.

His eyes landed on me, and I suddenly went cold. His expression never changed as he headed our way. Smaug stood next to the table and bowed his head.

"It is a pleasure to meet you. I never expected to have an Adisa grace my establishment."

His Welsh accent was thick as if he'd stepped right off the boat from Wales.

I forced a smile and found myself offering him a hand. I didn't know how else to greet him. By the way he gazed at me, the Adisa name seemed to hold such a reputation, I genuinely believed he saw my presence as a privilege.

"Not something I planned on doing when I woke up this morning."

He bowed his head again. "And yet, you did." His eyes wavered to my sister and Ric, who'd been quiet. "You bring friends. Pack, I presume."

I nodded. I decided honesty was the best policy. Perhaps, Kayla had been right about my instinct to be honest having more to do with being part Fae than my morals. I wouldn't give Smaug the entire truth but enough not to ask any more questions.

"I've recently discovered my ancestry background as a Fae and here I am. I didn't think bringing my over-protective mate in here would make anyone feel comfortable enough to answer questions."

There was a glint in his eyes that hadn't been there before. I'd said the magic words, giving him the indication that I'd need his assistance, and therefore an opportunity to sway me to the court.

"Aye. You certainly came to the right place. But we Faes do not indulge in sharing anything amongst others. Besides you, of course."

I read between the lines. "I am willing to sit somewhere private, as long as my pack can stay safely right here." I didn't expect him to hold back from playing any tricks, but I could at least hold him to not directly harming Braelin and Ric while we were here.

His smile was wide and furtive. "I swear it. Your pack will not have any physical or psychological harm done to them while they sit here."

I hadn't ignored the implication of them being potentially harmed the moment they stood from the table but took what I could get for now.

"I'll be a moment. Don't stand up," I ordered.

Braelin and Ric nodded in understanding.

When I slid out of the booth, I noticed Smaug's smile tightened, realizing I'd caught his trick of words. He chose to not say anything and guided me to a separate booth. All eyes shifted between me, and my pack sat four booths down.

Smaug sat across from me, waving one of his Fae servers over.

"A glass of wine for me and my new friend here."

A slender woman with freckles all over her face curtsied and disappeared before I had time to process what she was. She had slitted, pale green eyes and tiny sharp teeth that looked like it would hurt if she bit me. She was beautiful in a very exotic and alien way. A few seconds later, before I could ask what kind of Fae she was, the young woman reappeared with two glasses of wine in hand, placing them on the table.

When she turned away to give us privacy, there were two wings at her backside and my eyes widened.

"She's a pixie," Smaug explained. "They aren't always small flying creatures. Quite dangerous." He grabbed his glass and drank half the contents. "Anyway. For the purpose of you coming."

I nodded, looked at the wine offered and decided not to pick it up. Kayla said I wouldn't be affected but I didn't want to test that. But Smaug noticed and waited.

After a minute he frowned. "You come to my place of business, wanting information, only to not accept my hospitality. All I am asking is for you to share a drink."

He was right. *Fuck.* He certainly was good at persuading me and even though I came here with false pretense, part of me did want to learn more about my family name. He was clearly aware of it by calling me an Adisa.

I picked up the glass and I could have sworn the music in the restaurant got quieter as everyone waited to see me take a sip. I assumed they were wondering if my bloodline was strong enough to withstand the magic in their food and wine. If our plan was going to work, that meant I needed to take a risk.

Before I could talk myself out of it, I picked up the glass, bringing it to my mouth. I sniffed the contents, berries and oak aromatizing my nose. If there was any poison in it, I could not tell. Smaug watched in exhilaration as I let the wine fill me. I let out a breath when nothing happened, and he smiled. I tilted the glass, examining the wine further.

"It's delicious."

"My patrons' favorite," he agreed.

I doubted if it would be the humans' favorite if they knew what they were being served, but I wouldn't comment.

"What do you know about my family history?"

His lips pursed, humor dancing in his eyes like fire swirling from a breeze.

"You know, there's an easy solution to getting all the answers you need."

"And what's that?" I asked.

"Our Fae Queen, of course." His brows raised, waiting to be challenged in reference to me being under the Fae Queen's control.

There was a lot I wanted to say but held the words back, knowing it wouldn't get me anywhere.

"I don't know this Queen, and I have no desire to enter another realm. Coming here was hard enough but I figured since we are alike in a way, you'd advise me on what I need to know."

"Hm." Smaug finished his wine and placed the glass back on the table. I only looked away for a second and my eyes widened when he picked it back up, the glass filled with wine. "Being an Adisa is a gift. Your Fae kin have served under the queen for centuries, protecting our court and its people."

"Then why did my grandmother leave?" I wanted to see if he would avoid my question.

Smaug chose to respond, his answer different from I expected. "Because she blamed the Queen for her mate's death. But we Faes know that is not true. The wolf was weak and greedy. He expected power without earning and thought he was owed something. She took her daughters out of bitterness, which ultimately got all her daughters killed, leaving you as the last."

"And what happened to my grandmother?" Rachelle never explained what had happened to her and perhaps it's because she didn't know. But I wanted to know, if not for Rachelle, then for me.

"Your grandmother was punished. But that is not why you come. I know you must be curious about the Queen and her court. You want to bargain with her."

I tried not to show shock at how easily he had guessed what I wanted.

"And if I was, what would she want?"

He shook his head. "No. That is not how this works."

I narrowed my eyes. "Then what do you want?" Was I about to make a bargain with him? I had not prepared and considered my options. There was no turning back and I needed to improvise.

"Friendship." Smaug made it seem simple and I doubted that. Something about me being his friend would bring trouble for my life later on, but what else was new? I could have denied him but then he could get up and end our conversation.

"What does friendship mean to you?" I asked.

He gave me a sly grin. "Conversations where we share things that matter to another. Helping each other when in need. Sharing resources."

"So, you want me to spy and give you intel whenever you ask. Do your dirty work and allow you room to build power of your own in the court and off it?" I reinterpreted.

"So, you do know what friendship is? Good!" He finished his second glass and leaned back into his seat. "Do I have your friendship or not?" He asked. "And don't think it is easy to break a promise with a Fae, especially being Fae yourself, because it is not."

Unfortunately, I believed him and groaned. "Fine. Friendship."

"I'm very glad to hear." Smaug smiled gleefully.

"What does the Queen want more than anything if it doesn't mean I have to give myself up to her?" I asked.

Smaug lips pursed. "Your first born."

My eyes widened. "What?" I said more loudly than I intended.

"She'll let you go if you promise your first born to her," he repeated.

I snorted. "First, I don't have kids nor do I…" I had to think for a minute. I did want kids but that wasn't the point. "I'm not planning to have kids any time soon and even if I were, just…no!"

He chuckled. "You will have a daughter as it has already been seen. Two in fact."

"What?" I couldn't hold back my second outburst, finding his words ridiculous. "Neither you nor the Queen knows what my future holds."

"The Queen shared with us a vision of the future and you are a part of it. She only told us because she wants to make it clear that if you die by any of our hands, we are destroying our future and choosing death."

I couldn't hear any more and waved my hand for him to stop.

"I'm not giving away anyone connected to me so let's drop it and stop playing games. What does she want?"

Smaug frowned. "Set eyes upon her and you shall hear her desires through thought and choice."

Great. He was giving me riddles.

"How about you give me someone else to talk to who might know?" I asked.

"Like…?"

"Fenix," I said.

His eyes narrowed. "They don't respond to my calls, but I can take you to them."

Bingo. I held back a smile.

"Is it far?"

"Only a few steps." He made it seem so easy. I knew he was going to send me into a trap, but little did he know it was the other way around.

"Fine. But my pack doesn't leave my side."

Smaug tilted his head over and took in my sister and Ric, annoyed at the sight of them.

"Perhaps it's best if they stay right here."

"My mate will never allow me to go anywhere without them," I argued.

"Fine. But they stay at a distance from me."

I nodded and stood as he did the same, walking past Braelin and Ric without saying a word.

From the corner of my eye, I noticed the Fae who had first greeted us head toward the back where we were headed. I glanced at my sister and she stood, knowing it was almost time.

Ric got up a second later and followed behind as a few more Faes stood.

I didn't trust Smaug. I had two of my pack here, so if his plan was to force me through a portal, it would require an aggressive approach. But Rikki and the others would be waiting in the back and that meant a potential fight. I trusted in the plan and continued to walk behind Smaug as he talked about where we were headed.

The hall to the back was long and narrow and I realized there was no kitchen. That was odd. I could hear whistling in a riddling tune, building from a wall that appeared to be a dead end.

"Where are we going?" I asked, seeing no exit. "Shouldn't you at least let your people know you're leaving?" I was trying to stall.

I couldn't see how Rikki was going to reach me with no doors to give her access to me. I wouldn't panic and glanced back at Braelin. She had her eyes narrowed on Smaug, ready to fight.

I couldn't find the Fae that had walked back here, and I glanced around searching for him.

Smaug turned to face me with a furtive grin, lingering near the wall.

"You shouldn't worry about things that don't concern you. My establishment takes care of itself." His eyes darted to Braelin before looking back at me. There was a full body mirror alongside the wall, and I stared at it with confusion.

"It's a mirror." I twisted, perplexed by what he wanted me to do.

"No, it is a passage," he corrected.

I squinted my eyes expecting to see a shimmer or anything to indicate it was a portal, not that I knew what to look for. I took a step back, questioning what to do.

"Where does it lead?" I shifted a nervous glance at my sister, standing within arm's length. Where was Rikki? Discomfort sat deep in my stomach, a tingling feeling running up my spine. My throat was tight as I tried to talk. "You're not trying to trick me, are you?"

Smaug rolled his eyes and scowled in irritation.

"You wanted answers and I'm taking you to get them, unless you've changed your mind."

"Then you go first." I waved my hand out for him to move and when he didn't, I took another step away from the mirror, pressing my back against the wall on the other end.

"Fucking hell. I guess the werewolf half has you paranoid. Your kind is never trusting." Smaug crossed his arms and shifted his gaze back toward the front of the restaurant.

Braelin scuffed her foot against the floor, bored of standing around.

"We don't jump into portals without knowing where we're going. So, if you won't tell us then we'll leave."

"And I did tell you. You don't know how to listen with your ears, too focused on finding reasons to doubt me. I don't have time for this, so are you coming or not?"

He seemed really annoyed and I almost believed he was trying to help me but there was something about the way his eyes kept shifting back to the front. It made me turn to see what or who he was looking at.

That was my mistake. Smaug reached for me, thick strong fingers gripping my wrist as he pulled me toward the mirror. I was unable to slip away, my body lurching forward. My eyes widened as Smaug stood, half of his body through the mirror. It looked unnatural, the mirror only showing my reflection and half his body. He yanked me again and I repositioned my foot, leaning back to resist him but found it nearly impossible as if I were being vacuumed through.

Braelin reached for me, her arms curling around my body. I felt like the rope in a game of tug-of-war.

The skin around Smaug's eyes darkened, and I saw pure evilness as he sneered, using all the strength he had to pull me through the portal.

I screamed, terrified that if I went through, I'd never be able to leave. Just as hope began to slip away, I heard a loud thud on my left side where there was a dead end. A second portal had opened, the wall now black as if it led to nowhere but oblivion. Rikki leapt forward, fingers locking around Smaug's throat.

His eyes widened in shock, dropping my arm and I collapsed back into my sister's body. Braelin balanced me and I stood, before being shoved toward the new portal. Braelin ducked in time to avoid a sword angled to cut off her head. Ric was fighting for his life in the narrow hallway that seemed to have stretched further away from the front where we first walked in. The humans didn't seem to notice the violent fight, still dancing and singing to the music.

I stumbled into Kayla as she snarled and caught a Fae leaping out of the portal from the mirror. The blonde-haired Fae caught in Kayla's grasp reached out, desperate to reach me. The hall was too narrow to avoid the Fae's fingers brushing over my shoulder, only four feet of width to get away as I pressed my body against the wall opposite of where they stood.

Kayla twisted and slammed the Faes body hard enough to crack the wall right next to me and snarled. Her fangs were extended, and I watched her sink them into his jugular. The Fae screamed as Kayla fed from him savagely, his eyes dimming into empty vessels. When Kayla was done, she clamped her teeth deeper before yanking away a thick piece of flesh from his throat and spitting it out. Blood splattered onto her, and she licked her lips, watching him fall dead to the ground.

I stood unmoving in shock, never having seen such a viscous kill. I was relieved Kayla was on our side. It made sense that she was a vampire sister to Rachelle; they both had an absence of civility when it involved drinking blood.

Rikki had Smaug completely out of the portal, claws digging into his neck as she kept him close.

"Let's go," she ordered. She looked at me. "You go first."

Right now, Rikki was giving me an order as Alpha, and I'd listen. I turned and trusted where I would end up as I jumped through the portal they'd come through. It was only dark for a heartbeat before I stumbled into strong arms.

I looked up to find Shiloh holding me upright as I fought through the nausea.

"No time to breathe, hybrid," he teased. When his hand dropped from my shoulders I struggled to stand upright. He turned and pulled out two daggers as two more Fae came from atop the roof and leaped down with swords.

We were outside in the back parking lot of the restaurant. There were no cars and the humans that walked by along the street didn't seem to notice us. Shiloh bumped me backward and I staggered trying to collect my thoughts. He moved with such speed, defending himself and keeping me at a safe distance. The two Faes were fast too but not fast enough to avoid Shiloh's sharp daggers.

Rikki leapt through the portal, Smaug still caught in her grip. She moved away from the wall and looked off toward the street as an SUV sped onto the sidewalk.

Tato jumped out of the driver seat and lifted his hand up to signal for us to approach.

I didn't hesitate, running toward the SUV and climbing into the front seat as Rikki trailed behind, dragging Smaug's resistant body. Tato opened the back seat of the SUV in time for Rikki to toss Smaug inside and climb in after him. I turned to face the back as I watched Rikki pin Smaug into the cushion seats, his face a mix of pain and anger.

I turned, hearing shouting from the back end of the restaurant, seeing Rachel and her sister fighting alongside my pack and Shiloh. More Faes appeared, and I realized Smaug had been stalling to get his friends here to help take me. He hadn't expected to be the one captured. Tato hopped back into the driver's seat and Ric came to the other side just as Rikki yanked Smaug upright for him to sit in the middle.

Rikki turned, her face painfully close to Smaug's throat.

"Stop resisting or I will rip something off you, starting with your fingers."

Smaug stilled but didn't hide the scowl and disdain.

"My Queen will not allow you to get away with this."

Ric chuckled and patted Smaug's thigh. "We're counting on that."

"Let's go," Rikki ordered.

I could see Braelin and the others running to the Jeep as most of the Faes lay incapacitated on the concrete. Tato put the SUV in reverse, turned, and then drove off as if he'd been the getaway driver on multiple occasions.

When I finally let out my breath, we were a few miles from the restaurant. Smaug let out a string of profanity and threats, promising a gruesome death for everyone and a life of unpleasant servitude for me under the Queen's hand. I ignored it all, exhausted and hungry. Maybe I'd be scared later. Right now, I didn't care. I shut my eyes and let my wolf's hummed breathing help me fall asleep.

Chapter Thirteen

I woke up to Lloyd's face painfully close to mine and thought about punching him for startling me.

"You know, for a werewolf you sure do fall asleep easily," he said. "Did you even do anything to be this tired?"

I flipped him off and shoved him away to get out of the SUV. Rikki was taking Smaug into the garage where we had a cage inside, only used on rare occasions. The pack spilled out of the house, wanting to be updated on what happened but it had been an obvious success.

There was a lot we needed to address but my eyes drifted toward the shed, picturing the bed. Maybe Lloyd was right but who cared. I liked to sleep after a big task. Or workout. Or after a meal. I never noticed I slept too much, and Rikki never complained.

"What's next?" Rosemary came to me for answers, some of the pack doing the same.

I looked back to the shed and sighed. "I guess we'll wait. Rikki will know."

The Jeep pulled up beside the SUV as everyone else got out. Braelin came to my side and scanned me for injuries.

"I'm fine." I lifted my arms up and twisted in a circle so that she could have her thorough inspection. She wouldn't relax until she knew I was not hurt.

Our father came out, eyes darting between the both of us. It was still awkward seeing him here. I turned away as he approached, needing some emotional distance from him and everyone else. I told Braelin I'd stay close but needed time alone and walked off alongside the house. I could tell she wanted to follow me, but she let me leave without argument.

There was a lot of emotion coming from the pack. The anxiety of having an enemy within our territory made them frenzied and it was spilling onto me. There was fear of the Fae Queen coming here.

If I didn't take a minute to clear my head, I'd drop unconscious from sheer overload. Maybe that's why I was always so tired after a big ordeal. It took a lot out of me to sort through everyone's emotions, trying to maintain balance, and still manage my own thoughts.

I didn't go too far, finding a tree to hide myself from the line of sight. They'd know where I was by my scent but being invisible gave me some form of separation. I let out a slow breath and gazed up at the branches filled with dark leaves. It was cold and I could see smog coming from my breath.

My wolf was pacing inside, too much of the pack whining in my head. I squeezed my eyes shut and blew out harshly.

"Fuck!" I could feel them as if they were my own emotions. Some of the pack were scared and tears swelled around my eyelids. My hands shook violently, pure adrenaline pumping through my veins and knew it was a physical reaction to some of the pack's anxiety and rage. A taste of acid on my tongue made me want to snarl out in anger. Someone in my pack was dangerously close to shifting.

Inside my head I could see emotional auras pulsating like magical energies. Dark red and shades of green and purple. It was all too much.

"Be the one source of magic that flows through you. You are what keeps the pack's emotions grounded. Focus on what they need and extend it out to them." It was Shiloh. I could hear him close to me.

There was so much to feel but I listened to Shiloh's words. I couldn't figure out how to find my thoughts and reverse the built emotions coming from my pack. My Omega wolf seemed so distant from me.

"Hear your wolf's breathing and breathe with her," Shiloh guided me.

I squeezed my eyes shut and used my ears to listen. At first all I could hear was my pack's chattering and the wind blowing but as the seconds shifted to minutes, I could hear my wolf. She breathed deep and long, the sound comforting. I took a deep breath and found myself matching my wolf's intake and outtake of breaths.

"Now picture what the pack needs most," Shiloh whispered.

"Peace." It was easy to think of and I stuck to that thought. My wolf surfaced closer to me, the colors of my pack aura changing to one shade of clear green. My body began to relax, and I sighed in relief, opening my eyes. My surroundings seemed brighter as if the sun had finally come out. My Omega was in control, but my mind was present and awake.

In a low command, solidifying what I needed the pack to feel, I whispered, "Sleep."

I blinked and shut my eyes as the link I had with each member of my pack reverted to normal. I opened my eyes and looked at Shiloh.

He smiled and nodded.

"Bonnie!" Rikki yelled out my name. I could hear dismay in her voice.

My eyes widened and I quickly moved to the front of the house to find several members of our pack shifted into wolves and asleep on the ground. There were two more on the porch, and I guessed more asleep in the house.

Shiloh caught up and looked around in shock.

"Well, fuck me!" he chuckled.

"This isn't funny," Rikki sneered. "What the hell happened?"

"Uh…" I glanced around, not sure. "Um..." It seemed that was the only thing I could say.

"You told them to sleep," Shiloh said, snitching on me.

I turned and gave him a sharp glare that suggested he stay out of this.

"I didn't mean they had to fall asleep. Only for their wolves to rest." Seeing as my entire pack was asleep, I now realized I'd used the wrong words. "I didn't mean literally," I added.

Rikki stared, dumbfounded.

"Okay!" she grumbled, trying to process it all.

"To be fair, Bonnie was completely overloaded with emotions. If she didn't act fast, she would have passed out," Shiloh said.

Rikki nodded in understanding.

"I felt that and was going to come to you right after," she assured me.

Kayla and Rachel came out from the garage and glanced around in astonishment.

"Well fuck, Nina's an Omega but she'd never done this before," Rachel acknowledged.

"There's being an Omega. And being an Omega and Fae," Kayla whispered.

"You think this happened because of…" I didn't know how else to say it. I was also Fae. Only a quarter, but it seemed I was a big quarter.

Rikki sighed. "Omegas can calm a pack and change the energy in a room, but you can't force them to sleep," she explained. Rikki walked over to me, and I leaned in as she curled her arms around me. She could see my mind swirling again with anxiety.

"You are Fae and moon bound." Kayla spoke the words and they seemed to be all I needed to realize my fated reality.

I was something more like her. Different but of my own design. And the only person who knew how it felt to be split in two was the mother I never got to meet. Her mother was a Fae and father was a wolf and that left me.

I let out a slow breath and called to my Omega, eyes brightening and spoke to my pack. If I could get them to sleep, what else was I capable of doing? I now understood the significance of why the Queen wanted me and I could never let that happen.

"Wake," I whispered and felt them stir.

One by one, the pack shifted to human skin. No one said anything. They only stared at me with confusion but not anger as I expected. No one liked being under control and that's what I had done, but they could see it wasn't done intentionally and from the way they all stood relaxed, I assumed they were relieved.

"Patio. Everyone," Rikki commanded.

The pack moved toward the opposite end of the house as Kayla and her sister stood to the side. When Rikki faced them, she nodded.

"We can stay and help," Kayla offered.

Rikki offered her hand, and they shook.

"We have to finish this on our own, but we thank you for the time committed to assisting us and putting yourself at risk," Rikki said.

"Perhaps, we should discuss a more permanent alliance after you are finished," Kayla suggested.

"I look forward to that," Rikki responded.

"I hope your mate doesn't mind that I call her in the future. It would be nice to hear another woman's perspective on being mated to an Alpha and living as an Omega."

Kayla nodded. "She'd actually love that."

Rikki and I watched the sisters head to their car and drive off, leaving us alone.

"I'm sorry—"

"Hey!" Rikki cut me off and pressed her fingers gently against my chin before tilting my head up to face her. "This is scary now, but we will figure this out together. Who you are…" Rikki spoke with such emotion it stunned me. "What you are is a blessing. Do not dare judge or punish yourself for it."

I nodded and found myself crying. Goodness, I was such a crybaby. Tears seemed to slip from my eyes more times than I could count. I was never this emotional before I'd changed, but again maybe it was because I was so much more empathic. I blew out a shaky breath and grinned.

Rikki kissed my lips and pressed our foreheads together.

"Let's go figure out what to do next before this Queen comes knocking."

*

There was no grievance about compelling the pack into a slumber, but I couldn't acknowledge anyone yet, trying to accept what I had done. I'd gone beyond what an Omega could do and somehow tapped into my Fae ability. Being a hybrid meant more than having two supernaturals connected through bite or birth. It was being merged as one kind of supernatural with a blend of both parts of me acting as one.

"We're not mad." Rosemary slid into the seat next to me. I looked at her and she smiled sheepishly. "My wolf was going into a frenzy. Putting me to sleep was the best medicine you could give. Besides…" she lowered her voice, and I leaned closer. "We all seemed to forget, even me, that you are new to not only being a werewolf but an Omega. And we've never had an Omega to realize the stress we could put you through."

I reached over and squeezed her arm.

"Thank you. I needed to hear that."

"You were my friend long before you became my pack, an Alpha's mate, or my Omega." Rosemary leaned across her chair and kissed my cheek. It was warm and comforting.

She was right. We'd been friends long before my life had changed. I thought of the years I'd come into the hospital with a patient and she'd been there to crush Jr's heart every time he asked her out and we'd laugh until I saw her again. That all seemed so long ago.

"How long are we going to keep him locked up in there?" Germain asked. His bushy brows kneaded together, peeved to have a Fae in our territory. A mature black man turned in his early forties, he stood an even six feet with a burly muscular build and bald head.

I'd only spoken to him once, finding it hard to carry on a conversation since he came across as conservative and disinterested in getting to know me personally.

It was Toni who addressed Germain's question.

"He will stay until he no longer holds value." Toni stood, arms crossed over his chest, his go-to posture. "I'm not saying it's going to be easy having an enemy in our midst, but we will deal, as it is commanded by our Alpha."

Rikki tilted her head to acknowledge Toni's support and chose a less dominant approach, taking a seat. Everyone who was still standing did the same and the pack seemed to relax.

"For now, no one is allowed to enter the garage without permission. We have him here to force the Queen's hand. It would be a mistake to bring the battle to her doorstep and if we're going to face her or her Faes, I prefer it to be in our territory. We know this place. It doesn't have to come to an all-out brawl, but we'll plan for one."

"He's just one of many Faes. Why would she come for him?" Lloyd questioned.

"Because taking him shows that we're capable of taking others. The Faes don't want a war with the supernatural. And I mean all of us because they live with the mindset that they're above all other supernatural, werewolves and vampires alike. Even lesser Faes. She'll have to get him back or risk having a civil war within her court."

"I was doing some reading online." I'd flipped through my phone trying to compare what was true and fiction. "Are there two kinds of courts? The seelie and unseelie court?"

Rikki nodded.

"Which court does she lead?" I needed to know because after learning the difference I really hoped it wasn't the latter.

Rikki's grim expression left me dismayed. Fuck me. She didn't need to reply. The unseelie court was run by dark Faes that took pleasure in stealing, tricking, and torturing humans. There was a lot I didn't want to face; I pushed it to the back of my mind.

"How long do you think it will be before she reaches out or comes banging on our door?" Greenly asked.

"It could be in the next hour or day," Rikki admitted. "Truth is, I have no clue. But in the meantime, I want everyone to be cautious. If you are to leave pack home or go to your individual ones, let us know where you are and don't take unnecessary risks."

Collectively, the pack answered, "Yes, Alpha."

Rikki dismissed most of the pack, signaling for Toni and Tato to approach. They walked off through the house and I grabbed my bag of chips I'd been munching on.

"Shouldn't you be in that meeting?" Rosemary asked.

I exhaled in relief that Rikki hadn't asked me to join.

"Whatever I need to know she'll tell me later. But they're probably going over logistics. I'm learning, I don't need to be in every conversation as I do not know werewolf strategies."

Edward, one of my pack members who had challenged me during Rikki's capture, walked up from behind, overhearing our conversation.

"Finally learning your place, huh?" His green eyes loomed over me in judgment.

I frowned, not sure where that comment came from but decided to address it.

"You know, I never thought I was above anyone but I'm sorry you felt that way." I took a moment to think of more to say. Maybe it explained some of the pack's hostility towards me. It wasn't me being an Omega or mated to their Alpha that bothered them but my ignorance and how I came across because of it. "I respect everyone here and openly admit to knowing nothing. Honestly, I should have come to you all for advice and help and I didn't. I jumped straight into this pack acting like I could still be the Bonnie I was."

Some of the pack was listening. They kept their distance, but their eyes were on me.

"Out there…" I looked out into the sky. It was still daylight, but it was darkening. In November, night came earlier. I tried picturing my life before discovering I was a werewolf but couldn't without triggering some unhealed emotion.

I smiled. "Out there, I was a leader. I got to save lives and it was something indescribable. I had dreams and plans, and I knew who I was. Out there, I was fortunate." My smile faltered and I looked back up at Edward, not hiding my raw emotions. "And in here, I was trying to hold onto that, because the truth is, I don't know who I'm supposed to be anymore. I don't know how to lead without fucking everything up, and I'm certainly not saving anyone. If anything, because of what I am…I'm causing you all pain."

That was my truth, and I couldn't lie to myself about it anymore. I watched Edward's hardened expression soften. He bowed his head and walked away as if to ponder my words. I could see others in the pack take in my words, but they said nothing.

It was Rosemary who spoke. “You are figuring things out and the first step to doing that is acknowledging it. But don’t you dare think you aren’t saving or helping anyone. You’re just doing it differently. And I love every part of what you are.”

I stared into her eyes, searching for the truth behind her words. She wasn’t just referring to me being a werewolf but also Fae. I smiled and nodded as she leaned in to kiss my forehead.

“Thank you for that.”

Rosemary nodded and stood as my sister and Malcolm approached.

“I’ll give you three some privacy.”

By the look in both my sister and Malcolm’s eyes, they wanted to talk. I wasn’t in the mood for any more heart-to-heart talks but for my sister, I would sit and listen.

Malcolm grabbed a chair and placed it in front of us as Braelin sat beside me. His brown eyes were filled with so much hidden emotion I couldn’t tell what he wanted from me. His smile drifted as he gave Braelin one quick nod.

“I know it’s hard for you to see me and I don’t want to make things harder on you. You have a lot to deal with and I’m sorry I wasn’t the father you needed.”

I exchanged a look with Braelin before focusing back onto him, unsure of where this conversation was leading. I could admit, some strange part of me was angry with him.

“It’ll take time.”

“I’ve decided to leave after we’ve dealt with the Queen.” He’d spoken it as if it was written in stone.

My face drew into a hard blank stare, unable to process his announcement. I looked at Braelin. "Let me guess. You're leaving with him."

She frowned. "We don't want to go but I need time with him. It wouldn't be forever."

"You have an amazing pack and friends. And your mate loves you," Malcolm reminded me as if I didn't already know.

I snorted. "Don't patronize me."

"He's not!" Braelin defended.

I nodded. "So, you get your father back and now you're ready to go."

"He's leaving because he can see it makes you uncomfortable to be here," Braelin said.

"So, it's my fault." Before Braelin could argue, I waved my hand out, not finished. I squeezed my eyes shut before looking at Malcom. "I've been uncomfortable since I came nose deep and stumbling into this world, and not once since I've had a clear understanding of my new life, have I decided to run or give in to discomfort," I growled. "But clearly you aren't father material because if you were, you wouldn't have walked out on your daughter." I pointed at Braelin and continued. "She might not tell you, but she was broken when you left her. You had your reasons, but she would have preferred to at least understand why you dumped her. Then you abandoned our sister, my mother," I snarled even louder, gaining attention from the pack.

From the corner of my eye, Rikki stood atop the patio watching, giving me the space to get my words out.

"And then, even when you had your perfect family again, you abandoned me. Do you see the pattern I've noticed? Why is it hard for me to trust that you'll stick around?" I laughed but there was nothing funny. "And here we are now. Because I'm not opening my arms up to you, it makes you so uncomfortable, you want to leave."

He sat there in shock.

I turned to my sister. "You know, I'm not angry with you. All you have talked about was father this and father that, as if he were some saint who didn't mean to leave you behind." I didn't know how to leave out my sarcasm. "Aren't you tired of being disappointed by him? Afraid he'd abandon you again? Have you ever thought that's why you haven't let Jr in, or anyone who could possibly love you? Hell, you aren't nearly as open to the pack as you should be." When Braelin's eyes widened and filled with tears, I brushed my hand over her cheek. "You're my sister and I will support whatever decision you make and always be here for you. Always."

I stood and looked down at the man who wanted to be my father but didn't know how to.

"You leave. Don't come back."

I walked off, leaving him to ponder.

When I made it up to the porch, Rikki asked, "Will you be okay?"

I shrugged. "In time. For now, I'm going to go check on Raine and her future cub."

Chapter Fourteen

It was quiet when I reached the room Raine had been staying in. I knew she was inside, hearing two heartbeats on the other end of the door. Raine's pregnancy hadn't started off on a positive note, being tricked and forced into an illegal clinic where the rogue werewolves planned to take her unborn cub. The woman who ran the clinic had her heart in the right place, but she'd gone about it all wrong. I'd invited Raine to stay here and join our pack and she'd been adjusting to life well, ever since. But I'd noticed a connection between her and Shiloh and hoped my instincts were right. They both deserved happiness.

I knocked gently and waited but didn't get an answer.

"Raine," I whispered. If she was sleeping, I didn't want to disturb her, but as I listened, I could hear her heartbeat quicken and knew she was awake. But I also smelled fear.

I opened the door to find Raine standing motionless as if caught in a mind snare and unable to shake herself awake. I walked further into the room, cautiously. When I noticed what she was staring at, I stiffened.

Raine stood like a statue staring into the full body mirror hung on the closet door. Her eyes looked as if she was seeing something more than her reflection.

I brushed my arm against her, but she didn't react.

"Raine," I whispered, this time with a bit more fear in my voice. I waved my hand in front of her face, hoping that would snap her awake but nothing happened.

Rikki must have felt my anxiety and rushed into the room. "What's wrong?"

I turned to answer but heard a laugh. It was masculine and yet soft and melodic, reminding me of someone. Before I could grab Raine, hands reached through the mirror and snatched her from us.

I screamed, leaping instinctively toward the mirror only to find myself pulled through.

*

I landed flat on my stomach, my face planted against a smooth cold surface. My mind swirled like I'd been sucked in at warp speed. Gravity felt stronger here, attempting to lift my body. Uncertainty surrounded me in a dreadful way, and I knew I was in what Kayla described as another realm.

I didn't get the chance to look up as I stilled from the sound of deep guttural snarls hovering over my body. My heart drummed loudly in my ears, and I curled my fingers into a tight fist. My body stiffened and I let out a shaky breath, feeling something large breathing against my neck.

I heard a whine and knew it was Raine. I squeezed my eyes shut and let my wolf out as my heart thudded more loudly. My wolf called to me, telling me to face what was above me. Before I could cower, I twisted onto my back and was met with cherry-red glowing eyes. Its breath smelled of chilled smoke and death.

I heard a whistle, and the monstrous beast took a few steps back, no longer hovering over me. It resembled a hideous version of a large greyhound, with bulkier shoulders and a wilder mouth. It looked to weigh more than 400 pounds; it's wide build muscular. The beast possessed an oddly human-like visage with a protruding nose in place of a muzzle. Its ears were short and pointed outward like the Faes back at the restaurant.

Its long thick claws scraped the smooth surface as it watched me with an obedient stance. I rose on my elbows to finally look around without turning away from the beast.

There was open fire on each of the fourteen granite columns, lighting up the entire throne hall and coating everything in an orange glimmer. The illustrations of gods on the curved ceiling danced in the flickering light while sculptures looked down upon the mahogany floor of this ceremonious hall. It looked elegant but from the energy of the hall, I knew too much death existed here.

A sapphire rug ran from the throne down through the center and split into two paths leading out. Ribbon banners with ornate quilting hung from the walls. I laid just at the center of the throne hall, as a woman in all white stared down at me with a gleeful expression as if she'd caught a big prize.

Raine sat, curled to her side a few feet from me, a Fae standing over her with a sword in hand. My eyes darted from her to the beast, and I knew I wouldn't be able to reach her without this beast tearing into me.

"Why has the music stopped?" The woman sitting on the throne questioned, swirling her arms as if acting as a conductor for an orchestra.

More Faes lined the hall like guards, their faces stoic. I noticed a young woman looking exhausted, holding a violin. She was human and I could tell she hadn't wanted to be here but was trapped. It saddened me to think how long she'd been here, playing music for the Queen and her court.

I finally took in the Queen, aware that she was in control of the beasts and her Faes. She had red, oily hair slightly revealing a carved, radiant face and pointy ears. Glinting violet eyes, set gracefully within their sockets, watched impatiently as she waited for the young woman to start playing. The Queen looked younger than me, but from what Rachelle mentioned she was centuries older.

When the violinist began playing, the Queen's smile returned and stood clapping. Her posture was straight and poised as she swirled her hips, moving to the music.

"Perfect!" she cheered.

Even though she was smiling, I could feel an eerie coldness inside her as she returned her gaze to me. She stepped down from her throne and walked to the beast, playing with its ear.

"Such a beautiful pet, isn't he? Well mannered," she added. "Yeth hounds are very loyal to their masters. As are Adisas but..." she laughed lyrically and shrugged. "Sometimes, they forget their place." The Queen lowered her head to the yeth hound and kissed its nose. "But not this one. Very loyal." She glanced back down to me, violet eyes darkening. "I don't appreciate the game you and your mate played."

I tried to think of what game she was referring to but didn't have time to sort it out because I heard Raine cry out in pain.

The Fae that was standing over her grabbed Raine by the hair, yanking her up to her feet. Raine tried to shove him away, but he was too strong. He slapped her across the face.

I moved to run to her but felt a hard body shove me. I flew several feet in the opposite direction. I groaned, the yeth hound standing over me again. Blood seeped from my nose, and I smeared it away with the back of my hand.

"She's a foolish little fighter, isn't she?" I recognized that voice. They'd been the one to grab Raine through the mirror, a trick I now knew they possessed. I thought they'd need someone in our realm to pull us through a portal, but I was wrong. Fenix walked over and kissed their Queen on the cheek, then smiled down at me.

"You could have come willingly, and all of this would have been avoided."

"Not likely," I muttered, lifting myself back onto my elbows as I faced the hound, Queen, and Fenix.

"Someone should have warned you to not play games with the Queen," Fenix chastised. "We Faes are the trickiest of the supernatural. You take one of us and we take one of yours."

"Where is my child?" The Queen asked.

I stared dumbfounded. "Smaug's your son?"

She chuckled. "All Faes under my court are my children," she clarified. "I ask again, where is my child?"

"How about a trade?" It was the only idea I could come up with.

I felt magic swirl around her and stilled.

"Do not try and bargain with me unless you are willing to make a great trade," she said.

I sucked in a breath, knowing exactly what she wanted from me. I turned to see Raine still being held by the Fae, awaiting further orders. I couldn't let any harm come to her or her unborn child, but I wouldn't give myself up to her.

I was willing to negotiate. "What do you want?"

She clapped as if she'd been waiting for that question all evening.

"Easy, my child. For you to pledge yourself to this court and give loyalty to me, promise to serve until your last breath."

That was not happening.

I shook my head and snarled, "I won't do that."

Her face hardened and Fenix moved to stand over me, wearing an annoyed expression.

"My Queen has given you a kind offer. It would be foolish to refuse it."

I shrugged. "I refuse it."

Fenix leaned down and slapped me across my face. I hadn't expected it to hurt so badly but Fenix clearly had supernatural strength. They stared down at me as if I were garbage.

"The Adisa promised loyalty to the Queen, and it is your duty to answer that call."

"My name's Bonnie Collins," I snarled through gritted teeth. "Perhaps it's time to end that contract and move on. You clearly have more than enough servants."

"But not an Adisa!" The Queen screamed like a child having a tantrum. "You were promised to me as your children will be. And your children's children," she sneered.

I could feel my wolf pacing inside, screaming *no*! I wouldn't allow the Queen, or anyone, to dictate my future or my children's future. I closed my eyes, trying not to act irrationally. Slowly, I scooted away and stood, no longer finding myself weak enough to have to sit below them. I stood tall and confident. In the back of my mind, I could hear Rikki cheering me on and telling me to win.

But somewhere beyond the depths of my consciousness, I could also hear Rachelle telling me what to do. In some way, we would always be linked through the cursed bond she had with my bloodline, and I found comfort in that.

But that voice in my distant mind grew and I began to think Rachelle was really speaking to me. I smiled when she whispered the words I felt confident saying.

"I am announcing in front of an open court a bargain with the Queen."

Every Fae's pointy ears perked up, hearing the official offer of bargain. The Queen grimaced but inclined her head in acknowledgement.

I closed my eyes and thought of the words Rachelle had been whispering in my head and my breath caught. I glanced back at the Queen and spoke.

"My bargain is to challenge the Fae kin that caused my bloodline to become indebted to you. As my kin could not fight the Faes who'd nearly wiped us out, I pledge to regain our independence by doing so now."

The Queen's eyes widened in shock. "How do you know those Faes responsible are still alive?"

"Because, if they weren't, my grandmother wouldn't have still been serving you. She would have reclaimed the home of her mother and all the mothers before she lost." I looked at her with deeper understanding. Everyone kept mentioning I was of a strong bloodline, and I now could see what that meant. The Adisas had been a strong independent people with their own royalty. It made sense now. To have another royal bloodline beg for her, it boosted the Queen's ego and made her feel far superior than she probably was.

"You must be smart if you've figured that out. But I have a strange suspicion someone's feeding you information." The Queen watched me with careful eyes.

She wasn't wrong. Rachelle had been using her magic to relay messages to me. Rikki had probably gone to Rachelle and told her of me being taken to the other realm. But I was sure Rachelle knew the moment I'd arrived here.

"What do I get out of this bargain?" she sneered, snapping me from my thoughts.

I considered and knew I had to give her something of equal value or it wouldn't be a proper bargain. My words also needed to be careful as she could manipulate the bargain with insinuations. I wouldn't like that and nor would Rikki, but it had to be fair, and this would only be temporary.

"Until I can rewrite my Fae kin's path and regain status as an independent, I will…" I sucked in a breath, her eyes widening with eagerness I hated to see. Even now, she believed I wouldn't succeed, and I knew she would make it hard for me to do so. A thought came to me as I continued. "I promise to swear service to you, outside of the court until the very second my kin's status is regained, with no hindrance from you, yours, or any who would assist your court, and the understanding that I will only assist with matters that cause no harm to anyone, including all I deem pack, family, and friends." I knew I had to say my bargain in one whole sentence so that she could not easily separate my words and use them against another.

If the Queen was shocked by my bargain, she didn't let it be seen but her body stiffened. I knew it was a good bargain. I could see she wanted to refuse but to do so would be foolish, since there would be no better bargain than that. A malicious smile curled her lips as she chuckled.

"She is more Fae than we all expected. Very cunning," she complimented. Letting out a breath, she continued. "I counter the bargain by adding a timeframe." She grinned.

I swallowed, realizing the mistake I'd made, but it was too late. She saw my fear and her smile deepened.

"I give you six months to regain status and if you don't, your bargain will be dissolved, and you will pledge loyalty to me."

"A year?" I challenged. She couldn't expect me to find out who took my Fae kin's status, nearly wiping us out and regaining control in less than a year. I still didn't even know what kind of Fae I'd come from.

She gave Fenix a look and they nodded.

"One year to this very day!" she replied.

Fuck. One year. I could do this. Besides, I wasn't alone.

I nodded.

"Excellent," she cheered, no longer playing the serious Queen.

She clapped her hands and a small man, no more than four feet, wobbled our way. He was stocky, with a long beard with gray eyes. I smiled awkwardly as he bowed his head. I realized he was a dwarf.

"My Queen!" he chimed, holding out a long canvas style paper.

"The bargain has been made, now all that is left is to sign it," the Queen said.

This was official. The dwarf pulled out a small dagger and handed it to the queen. She sliced her palm open and lifted her hand up as blood spilled onto the paper. She handed me the dagger and I knew there was no way around this. Every Fae watched and I grimaced, slicing my palm open, flesh burning. She grabbed my wrist and shifted my hand over the paper as blood dripped down.

When she was satisfied, she let me go and I bit down a snarl.

"One year to this day!" she reminded me and the court. "Until then," she said, gleeful. "Be expected to return to my court the moment I call for your service."

"Fine," I bit out. "For now, I ask to leave with my human pack member beside me."

The Queen shrugged. "Fine by me, as long as my child is returned to me the moment you return."

"Agreed." I nodded. The Fae who'd been holding Raine let her go and she ran the rest of the distance to me. I grabbed her hand and squeezed tightly. "Just a few minutes more."

Raine's eyes were red from tears, but she nodded, looking braver.

The Queen studied me for some time before I noticed a black hole open on the floor. That was our way home.

"I will leave the portal open until my child is returned through it."

I nodded.

"You are free to go." She smiled as I moved closer to the portal. "And Bonnie. I look forward our time together."

That was the last thing I heard before Raine and I leapt into the portal.

Chapter Fifteen

The day after I returned, I'd wanted to see my mom right away. She'd been calling as if sensing the moment I came back and I knew her worry would only deepen if I didn't talk to her in person. I wasn't ready to think about the Fae Queen or my supernatural problems, for the first time ever preferring to face my mom's wrath.

I stood on the porch about to knock, knowing I was overthinking things. No matter where we were in our relationship, this would always be my home too. I opened the door to the smell of freshly baked biscuits and bacon. My mouth watered and I knew anytime my mom made those, it was her way of saying she loved me. Those were my favorite two things to eat, and I thanked her for it every time.

The house was warm, keeping the cold November air out, the living room decorated with new furniture she'd had for the past several years. It felt more modern and lively, as if for the first time since my father's passing, she was opening up to new possibilities.

"Mom!" I called out, not wanting to spook her. Since my change, I moved more silently, not something I did purposely. It was just predator instincts to not be heard until it was too late. I could hear her in the kitchen. As usual, I sucked at using my nose or I would have realized someone else was here too.

I froze, stuck in place from indecision as my brother Darnell stepped out of the kitchen. His brown eyes widened at the sight of me, his heart picking up in pace. It wasn't shock in seeing me but relief. My mom had clearly told him I was coming by, and he wanted to see me. He stood a few inches taller, his build bulky and muscular from his many hours spent weightlifting. He was tense and immobile as if waiting for me to run away.

Part of me wanted to but when my mom stepped out of the kitchen and ran to me, I knew I couldn't. Her arms curled around me, squeezing me tight as if thinking I would never return.

I couldn't help but tear up, hugging my mom back. Rikki had offered to come with me, but I knew I needed to do this on my own.

"Hey, Mom," I whispered in her embrace.

She cried until she was satisfied that I wouldn't disappear again and loosened her grip. Her eyes met mine, furious at me but also loving.

"You scared everyone. Even that partner of yours. She tried to hide it, but I saw her fear when you left."

Rikki had told me what she'd shared with my mom, so I tried to stay on script.

"Yeah, sorry mom. I just…I needed to face some things." I tried not to notice Darnell's watchful eyes as he knew what really happened. He'd been enthralled by Jaleel and brought to me as a bargaining to force my hand. I smiled meekly as my mom leaned in and kissed my cheek.

"Come eat." She whisked me to the dining room, and I sat at the table, my brother on the other end. Freshly made biscuits and bacon were already on the table, along with shrimp and grits. She took her seat beside me and patted my hand resting on the table. "You look so tired, honey. You need to rest."

I nodded. "I know." She had no clue what I'd been dealing with in the last few days, but I was far from ready to tell her about that. I stared down at her hand still lingering over mine and smiled. The fact that she hadn't let go told me she suspected there was much more I was keeping from her, and I hated it. The secrets. Lying to her about my entire new life.

Darnell just watched me. When our eyes met, he smiled, and I could see that it was genuine. I frowned, not sure how to feel about that and looked away. Werewolves had the instinct to either be the dominant or the less dominant, but I was an Omega and neither held value to me.

"Oh, I forgot." My mom got up and rushed to the kitchen.

I smiled.

"You look…good." Darnell clearly didn't know what to say.

I tried to entertain the conversation by responding. "I'm alive."

His brows furrowed and he averted his head, angled down at the table.

"I'm sorry. For it all."

Despite the anger I wanted to let out at him, I believed him and was too tired to fight. I'd been through enough.

"I know you are," I said.

My mom came back with a pitcher of freshly squeezed orange juice and placed it at the center of the table.

"Did your brother tell you? Devon's tour is finishing, and he'll be home in a month."

My oldest brother, and technically my nephew, Devon had been in the military for the last fifteen years and we barely spoke to each other before and after he left the first time he joined.

"That's great, Mom!" I said, happy for her. I wasn't ready to figure out what that meant for me.

We ate in silence for a few minutes, and I could tell there was tension building from my mom's tense posture. I knew this wouldn't be just a quick and happy visit. She wanted to know the truth.

I put my fork down and sighed.

"I'm sorry, Mom." She only sat quietly, waiting for more to be said. I couldn't tell her everything right now, but I could give her something. "There's so much that's changed, and it happened so fast that I think I'm barely learning how to live with it all." I reached out and held her hand resting in her lap. "Mom."

Her gaze lifted, tears right at the surface.

"I know something's different. You are my daughter. I'm not blind."

I sighed and nodded. I thought of Rikki and the pack. My new life as a werewolf and an Omega. Braelin, Malcolm, and even Rachelle. The secrets of my Fae linage and the Fae Queen. There was so much to tell but I needed to figure out how to tell her. It wasn't something I could blurt out.

"Give me a month," I said.

Her eyes widened.

"Give me some time to figure out a few things and I promise, Mom, I'll tell you everything."

She studied me for some time, forming a conclusion and she smiled.

"One month!" she said, adamantly.

I frowned.

"One month, Bonnie. I think that is more than enough time to figure out how to pretty up your words in order to feel safe telling me. But know, no matter what you share with me, I will always love you and never turn my back on you." She smiled and it left me with so much hope.

"Okay, Mom. One month," I said. I watched Darnell smile too and knew he was relieved that I planned to tell her everything. He didn't know everything either, but I supposed it would be easier telling her with him there to support our mom. I didn't know if my relationship with Darnell would ever get better but by the look of hope in his eyes, I could see the possibilities.

Hard conversation out the way, we went back to eating, until I needed to leave to go back to the pack and my mate. Our troubles weren't over, and Rikki would send the entire pack here if I wasn't home before dark.

*

A week had passed since leaving the Fae Queen's court. After returning home through the portal and giving Smaug back, I'd shared everything, leaving Rikki stunned by the bargain I had made. She hated it, as expected, but I knew she understood my dilemma and knew it was the best choice to make. It hadn't been my intention to go through the portal as I had promised not to leave on my own again, but she knew I couldn't have left Raine to suffer at the hands of the Fae Queen.

We had one year to figure out my Fae kin history and regain my status. My gut told me the Queen knew the very Faes responsible for nearly wiping my kin out and leaving us on our knees. If I'd learned anything from the

Queen, she'd probably been the one to assist with the Faes' slaughter of my kin.

The pack tension had been at a peaceful level, no longer expecting Faes to show up unexpectedly. The Queen said she'd call for my service and I had no doubt she would.

I mentally planned a day to return to the caves and talk to Rachelle, sensing she knew a lot more about my kin. She had been in love with my grandmother after all.

I was taking a bite from my taco when Malcolm walked up to the kitchen counter. Jr had been coming by to cook for the pack. I was proud of him for being consistent in trying to prove his worth and dedication to being a part of the pack. I had pictured Jr as a werewolf and found myself excited for the future if Rikki decided to turn him.

I put my taco down, using a napkin to wipe my hands. I peeked behind me and found that everyone had cleared out of the kitchen. I prepared to hear him announce he was leaving and stood, not giving away anything that would suggest how I felt.

"I wanted to say that you were right." Malcolm placed his hand on the counter and then fisted it, having second thoughts about reaching to clasp my hand. "I have failed all three of my girls and I was about to do it again." I watched as his eyes lifted to mine, honest and timid.

I wanted to see and feel everything Braelin had for this man. The man who raised me could never be replaced but I craved to know this man too. He helped create me with a woman I'd never meet but whom he could tell me about. I could see our similarities. My skin was lighter, probably from my birth mother's mixed race, but I had his cheekbones and nose and the color of his eyes.

He was a strong black man who'd been dealt a hard life, but he stood before me now as if surrendering for the first time. To what, I had no idea.

"I spoke with Braelin and she told me you meant every word. You told me off and I thought…wow, that's my daughter. So fierce and outspoken. I certainly had no part in your life and never would if I left again now." He finally worked up the courage to touch me as his hands closed around mine. "I'll never find happiness if I keep making excuses for not being a father. So, I won't run. You continue to take things as slow as you want, and I'll work every day to prove why I should be both your father and your sister's father. That's if you decide to tell her too."

He was referring to my mom. She'd always be mom no matter how our DNA lined up, but she deserved to know. I'd gone to see her the day after my trip to the Queen's court. My mom popped me on the arm for scaring her and she'd asked for the truth.

I promised I'd explain and asked for time, and she'd given me a month. That was my mom. She'd taught me to be honest and outspoken.

"I'm working up the courage to tell her, but I plan to. I think it's best to start with me being a werewolf first since she wouldn't believe you were her father otherwise. I mean…you look younger than her."

"That makes sense. I've waited this long. I could wait however long you need." He smiled, the silence between us comfortable. "Can I stay?"

I looked into his eyes and held back from replying right away. I'd told him he could stay the first time for Braelin but now, I had to make that choice for myself. I studied his eyes, trying to see beyond the flesh of a man who'd left me in the care of his daughter. He had kind eyes that still held youth. Could I call him dad one day? I didn't know the answer to that, but I wanted to believe I would someday.

"Stay."

*

Rikki had been out on town business all day when she decided to return home for the evening. She thought it was time to buy more land since the family that owned about five acres put their house up for sale. We weren't too close to our neighbors for any humans to ever hear what went on, but I think living next to people they got nervous around anytime they bumped into us in town was enough to finally pack up their bags.

I had a bubble bath ready for Rikki when she came into our private home. Soft native music was playing in the background, and I had a bottle of chilled wine resting on the table next to sliced steak.

I stood beside the table and took a breath, finding my confidence. Rikki opened the front door and smiled, peeking in with curiosity.

Rikki's brows raised, surprised from the sudden change of scenery as I helped take off her coat and hang it. I had tulips in a small vase by our bed with candles everywhere I could put them, the only things keeping our place lit.

"What's the occasion?" Rikki grinned, watching wherever I moved.

I shrugged playfully. "Being in love and always staying that way."

I never wanted to make her feel second or unwanted again. I meant what I said about proving that to her for the rest of my life. I stood in a silk robe, her eyes watching me. I pulled it off to reveal I was wearing nothing but a pulse-racing coquette that mimicked a burlesque style, with crisscross satin ribbons running down the front of the basque. My breasts were pushed up, adding to the sex appeal I was trying to pull off. My hips were curved enough to showcase my hourglass shaped body, wearing a G-string. I thought I saw Rikki gulp and I smiled.

I'd never done anything like this before and she looked happy. Her eyes raked all over me and I reminded myself I had a whole night of spoiling her to do.

"Not yet. You are the main dish tonight."

Rikki laughed. Not just soft laughter but bent over, eyes watering laughed. I think she was on the verge of going into shock from what I was wearing alone.

Out of everyone, it was Greenly and Rosemary who'd gone shopping with me at Victoria's Secret. I wasn't a super girly girl but tonight I could be, and any night Rikki desired. I'd shaved, waxed, and gotten a pedicure and manicure for tonight. Braelin had curled my hair and it sat perfectly around my face, with light makeup applied.

"First, you have a bubble bath calling your name," I announced. "The pack already knows not to bother us for anything."

I helped undress her until she stood naked and got her into the tub.

Rikki slid inside and perked her eyes up when I came back with a tray of meat and wine.

"Do I get you too tonight?" She asked, eyes dipping down to my breasts.

"After I have you first."

She licked her lips and nodded as I fed her meat. A werewolf's favorite meal. She sipped on her wine, and I moved to the backend of the tub and began massaging her stiff neck. Rikki groaned and I felt her relax more than she ever had, her arm draped lazily over the edge of the tub.

I took the empty glass from her and placed it on the counter.

"What's your plans for the new property?"

Rikki groaned but managed to get words out. "I want to expand everything by building a few more homes. Creating our own safe community. We need more wolves. But we also need a safe place for future guests and allies since we do live an hour or more from most of them."

"Mhmm. I love that." I continued to listen as I massaged my way down her shoulders.

"I spoke with Kayla, and she'd like to organize a yearly summit. We all have challenges and enemies who hop from city to city, state to state. If we could learn to communicate more, we might be able to defend our people better. Share resources. One day, we might need each other."

"That's a beautiful idea." It could be the start to new connections we needed in finding out the truth about my family but also providing more safety. "Does that extend to more than werewolves?"

Rikki nodded lazily. "Kayla is a vampire too, and you're also Fae. Plus, there's Amber and her people. It will be for anyone willing to have an alliance. We don't own the biggest amount of land compared to Kayla, but we are more secluded, and the temperament of weather is easier for vampires out here, so we were thinking of hosting the first one here."

"What date do y'all have in mind?" I slid back to her side and waited for her to open her eyes.

"Two months." Rikki opened her eyes and reached out to brush her hand along my jaw. "This can change our future. Open the door to new opportunities. I want our pack to succeed and flourish. And I want it to happen with you standing beside me."

I leaned into her hand and sighed.

"And we will," I whispered before leaning in to kiss her.

The kiss was soft and polite but promised more. When I pulled away, I grazed the tip of my finger between her breast before cupping one. Rikki moaned and pressed into my hand, stealing another kiss.

She moaned against my mouth and shuddered when I began playing with her nipple. I wanted to put it in my mouth and suck hard but held back a little longer.

"Tonight is about us and our future and how much I love you. But tonight, I want you to give in to me completely. Do you understand? Tomorrow, we fight for a better future for our pack."

Making love to Rikki was always magical but I knew we could give more. Feel more. We were no longer new mates trying to discover each other. We'd had time to build on our love and learn what each of us needed. No, tonight would be more than about sex. It would be about solidifying our future together with no room for anyone to ever come between us again.

"Tonight, is about us," she agreed.

I smiled, understanding something now that I hadn't before. Words Rikki uttered to me once. At the time, I cringed when she spoke the words, still thinking like a human.

But as my lips moved in to claim hers, I silently made a promise with my wolf in agreement, to always fight for Rikki. And even kill for her and the pack. And do it gladly.

About the Author

Domina Alexandra is a native of Southern California and currently lives her life as a nomad, never sure of which state she'll land in next. She is an author of stories with strong female protagonists, authentic emotions, and thrilling action scenes that mirror her past career as an EMT and Law Enforcement. Not to mention finding unique places that inspire her fantasy universe. She grew up writing poetry as an outlet, and in 2006 she joined a Live Theater program where she played many roles in a production of plays and musicals. During her four years of acting, she fell in love with writing monologues, screenplays, and storytelling. When Domina's not writing or finding new things to explore, she's soaking her feet in the dirt to ground herself, running wild with her dog, Carson, and rewatching her favorite movies and TV shows.

Other Titles Available From Triplicity Publishing

A Rogue's Redemption (Rogue Series book 1) by Domina Alexandra. Forcibly turned into a werewolf, Danni's life has been trapped by her creator for years, until the Sentinel of a Sacramento pack finds her in a fighting pit next to a couple dead wolves. As the pack's Sentinel, Karissa doesn't get much respect for her position. When she busts an illegal fighting pit in her territory and finds a werewolf with a power far greater than she's ever seen, she realizes she's not only found her one true mate, but she'll have her role as Sentinel questioned now more than ever. Before Danni and Karissa can navigate through the murky waters called emotions and thoroughly explore their emerging bond, they will have to face a set of challenges. With an unsupportive pack, an illegal fighting pit, and an annoying trespasser who wants Danni back, there will be no room for error. Secrets, feelings, and a whole lot of intense staring at lips will keep even the most modest readers on edge in a new series called: *Rogue.*

New Beginnings by Graysen Morgen. Captain Tristan Malloy has dedicated her life to the Army and takes her job very seriously. When an unexpected situation arises back home, her world is upended. When the dust settles, she makes a choice that will change her life forever. Courtney Hewitt is a third generation Army helicopter pilot, who's been flying in and out of war zones until she gets sent to South America for a Special Forces Operation. The redeployment is a welcomed change of scenery, and the leader of the special forces team she's assigned to work with is an added bonus Courtney can't wait to cash in on, until the alluring captain abruptly kicks her to the curb, ending their secret, torrid affair. When Courtney follows her home on leave and discovers the reason, she must make a choice of her own. Everyone deserves a chance at a new beginning in this action-packed romance.

An Omega's Grief (Claimed Series book 3) by Domina Alexandra. Bonnie's life is finally slowing down, but on a weekend getaway with her mate Rikki, things quickly turn sour when a human is killed right in front of them. Worse, Bonnie has a stalker with an unimaginable power, and if she doesn't confront this dangerous individual, it might cost her pack and friends their lives. With time against her, Bonnie will have to make her toughest decision yet.

Crossed Reins by Graysen Morgen. Barrel racing is Carly Rae Walsh's life, until it's ripped out from under her. With nothing to do and nothing to lose, she uses her years of horse whispering skills and intuition to train a troubled thoroughbred racehorse. Allison McKinley is a world class dressage rider who has stepped back from the spotlight to mourn the sudden death of her mother. The last thing she needs when she decides to start training again for competition, is her father's impulsive desire to own a racehorse, and his bizarre decision to choose a rodeo barrel racer as the trainer. The two women have nothing in common except horses, and even that's a stretch. Can they uncross the reins long enough to see what's happening between them?

Outside In by Breanna Hughes. Cali Evans is a survivor. Her life hasn't been easy, but her late father raised her to be smart, tough, and dependent only on herself and her wits. On the eve of her 21st birthday she meets Owen Bray - a beautiful and intriguing young doctor who equally frustrates and captivates Cali. That fateful meeting inspires Cali to make a better life for herself. The next day, hoping to make positive change, Cali hops a bus for the West Coast but never reaches her destination. Instead, she wakes up in an underground bunker with no recollection of how she got there. Upon her arrival, she learns that she's one of just forty survivors of a fast-spreading environmental toxin and that human life outside of the bunker has ceased to exist. Tired of the vague explanations and half-answers coming from the people in charge, Cali takes it upon herself to investigate the real reason why she's there and begins to uncover the sinister truth.

I Love You, Nora Whispered by Kathy L. Salt. Love in the time of horses and polio. England, 1948. Nora Lakes suffers from post Polio Syndrome and very low self-esteem. When her sister Martha manages to get her a job at Waterhouse Acre Stables, she can hardly believe it. She had never imagined that anyone would employ her, damaged as she is. She also never imagined she would meet anybody like Katherine. Katherine Waterhouse was born with a silver spoon in her mouth. She has a mean streak and doesn't like people in general. What she does like, is horses. She wants to be a professional rider but growing up in a conservative house where her choices are limited by her sex, Katherine has always been trapped in her role as a woman. Nora and Katherine - two women with very different backgrounds, drawn to each other with an intensity neither of them is prepared for. Do they stand a chance?

Omega Rising (Claimed Series book 2) by Domina Alexandra. A few months of peace. That was all Bonnie Collins was granted. New trouble has surfaced and go figure, this trouble came with a new pair of claws. When an unknown pack comes to town, Bonnie is forced to make tough decisions that will influence her pack's future. Things only get harder when her mate is taken, leaving Bonnie in charge of a pack who still doesn't trust her. With chaos all around, it will be exactly what Bonnie needs to finally embrace what she has become. An Omega Rising. Book 2 of the *Claimed Series*.

Loose Ends by Joan L. Anderson. After her estranged sister is killed when she falls onto the subway tracks in Paris just as a train arrives, Allison goes to Paris to deal with her sister's body and collect her things. But, after talking to the police about the accident and viewing the subway surveillance video, something seems odd about her death. When Allison's hotel room in Paris is broken into with only a few things taken, but not any money or credit cards, she begins to wonder if it really was an accident that killed her sister, or if it was murder. Once Allison returns to Washington, D.C. to handle her sister's affairs, she soon realizes that her sister had been living a secret life and wasn't the person she had always thought she was. As troubling things begin to happen to Allison in D.C., she starts wondering if she will be the next person to die.

Real Love by Graysen Morgen. Leigh Myer is a trauma nurse practitioner who is not happy going through the motions of her daily life. When a friend offers up her mountain cabin for a relaxing vacation, Leigh packs her bags. She's never been to the mountains and certainly never in heavy snow. A chance meeting with a fish and wildlife officer turns her idea of a quiet, relaxing vacation…upside down. Camden Gorely loves her job and loves the mountain she works and lives on even more. She's tired of having flings with vacationers who visit for days or weeks at a time, until she meets the elusive nurse from the city. Can Leigh stop running from her past and allow real love into her heart?

Enticed by Love by Lynn Lawler. Henrietta Bailey is a mysterious woman who has spent her entire life living in the town of Crescent, a sleepy beach community in central coastal California. She loves the beach, the ocean air, and the town itself. Her simple life fulfills her. However, she spends much of her time reminiscing about her long-lost love, a woman who left her devastated. Now, another woman awaits on the horizon; a wise, intelligent, and sexy lady who is sophisticated beyond her years. This woman yearns for her soul mate and lover. Will she be able to win Henrietta's heart, or will Henrietta be fated to live the rest of her days alone?

Love Undercover by Domina Alexandra. Remi Stone never expected to get the opportunity to work undercover for narcotics. But, when the chance arrives, she takes it. With drugs coursing through a high school, Remi has only until the end of the school year to find the suspects responsible. Undercover, Remi plays her role, moving one step further into the drug industry. She never thought she'd be moving one step closer to the woman who would change her life and take hold of her heart. There is just one issue. Remi Stone is undercover as an eighteen-year-old high school senior. And the woman she can't seem to ignore is her History teacher. There will be a lot of challenges along the way, including one that could cost Remi her life and her heart.

Playing the Game by Graysen Morgen. Randi Rojas is a professional soccer player who seemingly has it all, a successful career, a long-term girlfriend, a loving family, and a great group of friends…until a chance meeting with an attractive woman sends her way offside, and into a whole new game. Berkley Ward lives her life to the extreme, spending her days either in the gym or four-wheeling in the woods, and her nights patrolling the streets as an officer. Affairs with taken women are easy, but after years of playing games, she's finished…until she meets a beautiful woman and a game she can't resist. Both women play a dangerously seductive game of cat and mouse, teetering on the edge of friendship and affair.

Rebel Sweetheart by Sydney Canyon. When a headstrong, country music superstar starts getting threatening letters while on tour, her manager has no other choice but to hire someone to investigate the threats and keep her safe. Haley Nielsen is as stubborn as it gets. She does things her way, and her way only. The last thing she needs or wants is a babysitter following her every move and controlling everything she does. Shane Crowley isn't your typical private investigator, or bodyguard, for that matter. She's a former U.S. Deputy Marshal with a lot of experience, and an all or nothing attitude. Tempers flare and the energy burns red hot between the two women as they spend weeks together cooped up on Haley's tour bus, traveling the country. Will they stop resisting each other long enough to see eye to eye? Or will the letter writer make good on his threats?

A Tale of Spiders and Canned Soup by Kathy L. Salt. Living on your own can be hard, but even more so when you're dealing with haphephobia; the death of a twin sister; and a crush on your teacher. Mika is still in contact with her foster family who homes the loves of her life, three young children she would do anything for, when she begins attending University of Aberdeen and meets Pauline, an Australian that teaches Viking history. Neither woman is used to breaking the rules, and their way to each other is a hard one, especially when Mika vows to get custody of the children, whether she is ready to be a parent or not. *A story about growing up. A story about dealing with grief. A story about Mika and Pauline.*

A Night Claimed (Claimed Series book 1) by Domina Alexandra. Bonnie Collins had plans. And being a werewolf wasn't one of them. Attacked by a rogue who was out to claim her and facing what she now has no choice of becoming, Bonnie can't let go of her human life as a Paramedic. The last thing Bonnie needs is more challenges. However, Rikki, the Alpha of Mill City will be just that. Finding her to be possessive and ruling, Bonnie begins challenging the Alpha's every breath. Finding out her attack was no accident only makes her angrier at the situation. A group of rogues are out to get her. With no clue why, Bonnie has no choice but to seek help from the alluring Alpha and her pack, accepting the new world she was forced into.

Stunted by Breanna Hughes. Professional stuntwoman Jessie Knight takes her job very seriously and although she works in the entertainment industry, she has zero desire for fame or notoriety. She also has a very strict no-dating policy when it comes to coworkers. That is, until she meets famous actress Elliot Chase on the set of her new film. The adrenaline rush of the stunts is nothing compared to the sparks that fly between them. After a passionate night together, a sex tape is leaked that sends Jessie and Elliot's private and professional lives into a spiral. Will the fallout be too much for them to last? Or will they find a way out of the mess together?

Mission Compromised by Graysen Morgen. Natalia Moreno is thrilled when she arrives in Fiji for a relaxing vacation. However, she soon discovers the overwater bungalow she's staying in has been double booked for the entire stay, and the resort is full. Annoyed and frustrated, she has no other choice but to share her hut with a stranger. Christian Garnier is sent to Fiji for what she refers to as a working vacation, until she finds out she has an ornery roommate for the next two weeks who is dead set on making her job twice as hard. Soon, all hell breaks loose, and the two women are sent around the world on a wild goose chase.

Stargazing by Kathy L. Salt. Lissa stared open-mouthed at the GIF that played over and over on the screen in front of her. Heat flushed to her face, igniting her skin. Her heart started pounding in her chest. *Stupid internet, it should really come with a warning label.* She's never been interested in relationships or sex and as the years have gone by she has retreated more and more into her work.

Everything changes when she meets Star, a porn actress with a heart of gold and a troubled childhood. *They say that opposites attract, but how much of that is true? What chance do they have when one of them is a virgin and the other one star in pornography?*

I Belong with Her by Domina Alexandra. Tajel Pierce loves the thrill of being a paramedic. Every call she goes on gives her a rush. She makes no time for her personal life. No one can ruin her love for her career. Then there is Arianna Castaldi, who just transferred to her new paramedic position in a whole new state. All she needs is a new start without any distractions. Arianna and Tajel's relationship doesn't start off perfectly. Embarrassed of the one-night stand Arianna believes she had with Tajel, she wants to pretend they never met and make their relationship strictly business. The only choice they have to keep from strangling each other is to go from denying their feelings to accepting them as they work through intense 911 calls.

Awakened by Fate by Lynn Lawler. Jackie is a woman living life according to her own rules. She's married, but it's the unspoken, open kind. She can have as many female lovers as she likes; she just can't talk about them. After a bizarre encounter turns her world upside down, things slowly begin to change. She finds herself in desperation as she searches for answers. What she discovers is nothing is delivered in a neatly wrapped box. Now that everything has been brought out into the open, she finds she can't run away from her truth anymore. With her new life comes new responsibilities and a different outcome than what she was expecting. Jackie isn't alone in the story. She meets several new people who help her along her journey.

Nautical Delights by S. L. Gape. Lady Elizabeth Barrington has spent her entire life trying to please her family; constantly opting for a quiet life, she utilises her profession as a doctor to keep out of her families' clutches; bar the annual two-week Caribbean private cruise, where there is simply no budge. Confined to two weeks on board the Iconica super yacht, she intends on keeping her head down and enjoying as much of the holiday as she can, whilst keeping her family at arm's length. Until a crew member catches her eye.

Worlds Apart by S.L. Gape. Hollywood A-lister Heidi Spencer-Brady is everything you'd expect of an Idol. Loved by all, the British Beauty is graceful, talented, humble and so far removed from the 'typical' LA scene. When her husband's infidelity with his new 'leading lady' is leaked, Dawn, Heidi's best friend and manager, goes all out to protect her. She arranges for Heidi to go back to the UK and stay on her cousins' farm they had visited as children, much to the disappointment of the animal fearing Heidi.

Castor Valley (Law & Order Series Book 2) by Graysen Morgen. Jessie Henry is torn when she reads about the capture of the Doyle brothers, two young men who were part of her old gang. Unable to let them hang for a crime she's sure they didn't commit, Jessie leaves her wife and the Town of Boone Creek behind and sets out on a journey back to the one place she thought she'd never see again, *Castor Valley*. Ellie Henry watches the love of her life leave, not knowing if she will ever return. When she gets an odd telegram, nearly a week later, she fears Jessie is in trouble. With no other choice, she goes to the one person who can help her.

Fight to the Top by S. L. Gape. Georgia is a forty-year-old, single, Area Director from Manchester, UK who is all work and definitely no play. Having no time to socialise or spend time with her family she prides herself on being fit and well-polished. Erika is an Area Director for the same company, but in the United States. Whilst she is concentrating so heavily on the promotion she has been fighting for, she's starting to feel like her life outside of work is falling apart. The two women are exceptionally different, and worlds apart. Both of their lives are turned upside down when their jobs are snatched from under their noses, and they are suddenly faced with being thrown together by their bosses for one last major project...in Texas.

Boone Creek (Law & Order Series book 1) by Graysen Morgen. Jessie Henry is looking for a new life. She's unknown in the town of Boone Creek when she arrives and wants to keep it that way. When she's offered the job of Town Marshal, she takes it, believing that protecting others and upholding the law is the penance for her past. Ellie Fray is a widowed shopkeeper. She generally keeps to herself, but the mysterious new Town Marshal both intrigues and infuriates her. She believes the last thing the town needs is someone stirring up trouble with the outlaws who have taken over.

Witness by Joan L. Anderson. Becca and Kate have lived together for eight years and have always spent their vacation in a tropical paradise, lying on a beach. This year,

Becca wanted to try something different: a seven day, 65-mile hike in the beautiful Cascade Mountains of Washington state. Their peaceful vacation turns to horror when they stumble upon a brutal murder taking place in the back country.

Too Soon by S.L. Gape. Brooke is a twenty-nine-year-old detective from Oxford, who has her life pretty much planned out until her boss and partner of nine years, Maria, tells her their relationship is over. When Brooke finds out the truth, that Maria cheated on her with their best friend Paula, she decides to get her life back on track by getting away for six weeks in Anglesey, North Wales. Chloe, a thirty-three-year-old artist and art director, owns a log cabin on Anglesey where she spends each weekend painting and surfing. After returning from a surf, she stumbles upon the somewhat uptight and enigmatic Brooke.

Never Quit (Never Series book 2) by Graysen Morgen. Two years after stepping away from the action as a Coast Guard Rescue Swimmer to become an instructor, Finley finds herself in charge of the most difficult class of cadets she's ever faced, while also juggling the taxing demands of having a home life with her partner Nicole, and their fifteen-year-old daughter. Jordy Ross gave up everything, dropping out of college, and leaving her family behind, to join the Coast Guard and become a rescue swimmer cadet. The extreme training tests her fitness level, pushing her mentally and physically further than she's ever been in her life, but it's the aggressive competition between her and another female cadet that proves to be the most challenging.

Never Let Go (Never Series book 1) by Graysen Morgen. For Coast Guard Rescue Swimmer, Finley Morris, life is good. She loves her job, is well respected by her peers, and has been given an opportunity to take her career to the next level. The only thing missing is the love of her life, who walked out, taking their daughter with her, seven years earlier. When Finley gets a call from her ex, saying their teenage daughter is coming to spend the summer with her, she's floored. While spending more time with her daughter, whom she doesn't get to see often, and learning to be a full-time parent, Finley quickly realizes she has not, and will never, let go of what is important.

Pursuit by Joan L. Anderson. Claire is a workaholic attorney who flies to Paris to lick her wounds after being dumped by her girlfriend of seventeen years. On the plane she chats with the young woman sitting next to her, and when they land the woman is inexplicably detained in Customs. Claire is surprised when she later runs into the woman in the city. They agree to meet for breakfast the next morning, but when the woman doesn't show up Claire goes to her hotel and makes a horrifying discovery. She soon finds herself ensnared in a web of intrigue and international terrorism, becoming the target of a high stakes game of cat and mouse through the streets of Paris.

Wrecked by Sydney Canyon. To most people, the *Duchess* is a myth formed by old pirate's tales, but to Reid Cavanaugh, a Caribbean island bum and one of the best divers and treasure hunters in the world, it's a real, seventeenth century pirate ship—the holy grail of underwater treasure hunting. Reid uses the same cunning tactics she always has before setting out to find the lost ship. However, she is forced to bring her business partner's daughter along as collateral this time because he doesn't trust her. Neither woman is thrilled but being cooped up on a small dive boat for days forces them to get know each other quickly.

Arson by Austen Thorne. Madison Drake is a detective for the Stetson Beach Police Department. The last thing she wants to do is show a new detective the ropes, especially when a fire investigation becomes arson to cover up a murder. Madison butts heads with Tara, her trainee, deals with sarcasm from Nic, her ex-girlfriend who is a patrol officer, and finds calm in the chaos of police work with Jamie, her best friend who is the county medical examiner. Arson is the first of many in a series of novella episodes surrounding the fictional Stetson Beach Police Department and Detective Madison Drake.

Mommies (Bridal Series book 3) by Graysen Morgen. Britton and her wife Daphne have been married for a year and a half and are happy with their life, until Britton's mother hounds her to find out why her sister Bridget hasn't decided to have children yet. This prompts Daphne to bring up the big subject of having kids of their own with Britton. Britton hadn't really thought much about having kids, but her love for Daphne makes her see life and their future together in a whole new way when they decide to become mommies.

Rapture & Rogue by Sydney Canyon. Taren Rauley is happy and in a good relationship, until the one person she thought she'd never see again comes back into her life. She struggles to keep the past from colliding with the present as old feelings she thought were dead and gone, begin to haunt her. In college, Gianna Revisi was a mastermind, ring-leading, crime boss. Now, she has a great life and spends her time running Rapture and Rogue, the two establishments she built from the ground up. The last person she ever expects to see walk into one of them, is the girl who walked out on her, breaking her heart five years ago.

Second Chance by Sydney Canyon. After an attack on her convoy, Marine Corps Staff Sergeant, Darien Hollister, must learn to live without her sight. When an experimental procedure allows her to see again, Darien is torn, knowing someone had to die in order for this to happen. She embarks on a journey to personally thank the donor's family but is too stunned to tell them the truth. Mixed emotions stir inside of her as she slowly gets to know the people that feel like so much more than strangers to her. When the truth finally comes out, Darien walks away, taking the second chance that she's been given to go back to the only life she's ever known, but she's not the only one with a second chance at life.

Meant to Be by Graysen Morgen. Brandt is about to walk down the aisle with her girlfriend, when an unexpected chain of events turns her world upside down, causing her to question the last three years of her life. A chance encounter sparks a mix of rage and excitement that she has never felt before. Summer is living life and following her dreams, all the while, harboring a huge secret that could ruin her career. She believes that some things are better kept in the dark, until she has her third run-in with a woman she had hoped to never see again and gives into temptation. Brandt and Summer start believing everything happens for a reason as they learn the true meaning of meant to be.

Coming Home by Graysen Morgen. After tragedy derails TJ Abernathy's life, she packs up her three-year-old son and heads back to Pennsylvania to live with her grandmother on the family farm. TJ picks back up where she left off eight years earlier, tending to the fruit and nut tree orchard, while learning her grandmother's secret trade. Soon, TJ's high school sweetheart and the same girl who broke her heart, comes back into her life, threatening to steal it away once again. As the weeks turn into months and tragedy strikes again, TJ realizes coming home was the best thing she could've ever done.

Special Assignment by Austen Thorne. Secret Service Agent Parker Meeks has her hands full when she gets her new assignment, protecting a Congressman's teenage daughter, who has had threats made on her life and been whisked away to a Christian boarding school under an alias to finish out her senior year. Parker is fine with the assignment, until she finds out she has to go undercover as a Canon Priest. The last thing Parker expects to find is a beautiful, art history teacher, who is intrigued by her in more ways than one.

Miracle at Christmas by Sydney Canyon. A Modern Twist on the Classic Scrooge Story. Dylan is a power-hungry lawyer who pushed away everything good in her life to become the best defense attorney in the, often winning the worst cases and keeping anyone with enough money out of jail. She's visited on Christmas Eve by her deceased law partner, who threatens her with a life in hell like his own, if she doesn't change her path. During the course of the night, she is taken on a journey through her past, present, and future with three very different spirits.

Bella Vita by Sydney Canyon. Brady is the First Officer of the crew on the Bella Vita, a luxury charter yacht in the Caribbean. She enjoys the laidback island lifestyle, and is accustomed to high profile guests, but when a U.S. Senator charters the yacht as a gift to his beautiful twin daughters who have just graduated from college and a few of their friends, she literally has her hands full.

Brides (Bridal Series book 2) by Graysen Morgen. Britton Prescott is dating the love of her life, Daphne Attwood, after a few tumultuous events that happened to unravel at her sister's wedding reception, seven months earlier. She's happy with the way things are, but immense pressure from her family and friends to take the next step, nearly sends her back to the single life. The idea of a long engagement and simple wedding are thrown out the window, as both families take over, rushing Britton and Daphne to the altar in a matter of weeks.

Cypress Lake by Graysen Morgen. The small town of Cypress Lake is rocked when one murder after another happens. Dani Ricketts, the Chief Deputy for the Cypress Lake Sheriff's Office, realizes the murders are linked. She's surprised when the girl that broke her heart in high school has not only returned home, but she's also Dani's only suspect. Kristen Malone has come back to Cypress Lake to put the past behind her so that she can move on with her life. Seeing Dani Ricketts again throws her off-guard, nearly derailing her plans to finally rid herself and her family of Cypress Lake.

Crashing Waves by Graysen Morgen. After a tragic accident, Pro Surfer, Rory Eden, spends her days hiding in the surf and snowboard manufacturing company that she built from the ground up, while living her life as a shell of the person that she once was. Rory's world is turned upside when a young surfer pursues her, asking for the one thing she can't do. Adler Troy and Dr. Cason Macauley from Graysen Morgen's bestselling novel: *Falling Snow*, make an appearance in this romantic adventure about life, love, and letting go.

Bridesmaid of Honor (Bridal Series book 1) by Graysen Morgen. Britton Prescott's best friend is getting married and she's the maid of honor. As if that isn't enough to deal with, Britton's sister announces she's getting married in the same month and her maid of honor is her best friend Daphne, the same woman who has tormented Britton for years. Britton has to suck it up and play nice, instead of scratching her eyes out, because she and Daphne are in both weddings. Everyone is counting on them to behave like adults.

Falling Snow by Graysen Morgen. Dr. Cason Macauley, a high-speed trauma surgeon from Denver meets Adler Troy, a professional snowboarder, and sparks fly. The last thing Cason wants is a relationship and Adler doesn't realize what's right in front of her until it's gone, but will it be too late?

Fate vs. Destiny by Graysen Morgen. Logan Greer devotes her life to investigating plane crashes for the National Transportation Safety Board. Brooke McCabe is an investigator with the Federal Aviation Association who literally flies by the seat of her pants. When Logan gets tangled in head games with both women will she choose fate or destiny?

Just Me by Graysen Morgen. Wild child Ian Wiley has to grow up and take the reins of the hundred-year-old family business when tragedy strikes. Cassidy Harland is a little surprised that she came within an inch of picking up a gorgeous stranger in a bar and is shocked to find out that stranger is the new head of her company.

Love Loss Revenge by Graysen Morgen. Rian Casey is an FBI Agent working the biggest case of her career and madly in love with her girlfriend. Her world is turned upside when tragedy strikes. Heartbroken, she tries to rebuild her life. When she discovers the truth behind what really happened that awful night, she decides justice isn't good enough, and vows revenge on everyone involved.

Natural Instinct by Graysen Morgen. Chandler Scott is a Marine Biologist who keeps her private life private. Corey Joslen is intrigued by Chandler from the moment she meets her. Chandler is forced to finally open her life up to Corey. It backfires in Corey's face and sends her running. Will either woman learn to trust her natural instinct?

Secluded Heart by Graysen Morgen. Chase Leery is an overworked cardiac surgeon with a group of best friends that have an opinion and a reason for everything. When she meets a new artist named Remy Sheridan at her best friend's art gallery she is captivated by the reclusive woman. When Chase finds out why Remy is so sheltered will she put her career on the line to help her or is it too difficult to love someone with a secluded heart?

In Love, at War by Graysen Morgen. Charley Hayes is in the Army Air Force and stationed at Ford Island in Pearl Harbor. She is the commanding officer of her own female-only service squadron and doing the one thing she loves most, repairing airplanes. Life is good for Charley, until the day she finds herself falling in love while fighting for her life as her country is thrown haphazardly into World War II. Can she survive being in love and at war?

Fast Pitch by Graysen Morgen. Graham Cahill is a senior in college and the catcher and captain of the softball team. Despite being an all-star pitcher, Bailey Michaels is young and arrogant. Graham and Bailey are forced to get to know each other off the field in order to learn to work together on the field. Will the extra time pay off or will it drive a nail through the team?

Submerged by Graysen Morgen. Assistant District Attorney Layne Carmichael had no idea that the sexy woman she took home from a local bar for a one-night stand would turn out to be someone she would be prosecuting months later. Scooter is a Naval Officer on a submarine who changes women like she changes uniforms. When she is accused of a heinous crime, she is shocked to see her latest conquest sitting across from her as the prosecuting attorney.

Vow of Solitude by Austen Thorne. Detective Jordan Denali is in a fight for her life against the ghosts from her past and a Serial Killer taunting her with his every move. She lives a life of solitude and plans to keep it that way. When Callie Marceau, a curious Medical Examiner, decides she wants in on the biggest case of her career, as well as Jordan's life, Jordan is powerless to stop her.

Igniting Temptation by Sydney Canyon. Mackenzie Trotter is the Head of Pediatrics at the local hospital. Her life takes a rather unexpected turn when she meets a flirtatious, beautiful fire fighter. Both women soon discover it doesn't take much to ignite temptation.

One Night by Sydney Canyon. While on a business trip, Caylen Jarrett spends an amazing night with a beautiful stripper. Months later, she is shocked and confused when that same woman re-enters her life. The fact that this stranger could destroy her career doesn't bother her. C.J. is more terrified of the feelings this woman stirs in her. Could she have fallen in love in one night and not even known it?

Fine by Sydney Canyon. Collin Anderson hides behind a façade, pretending everything is fine. Her workaholic wife and best friend are both oblivious as she goes on an emotional journey, battling a potentially hereditary disease that her mother has been diagnosed with. The only person who knows what is really going on, is Collin's doctor. The same doctor, who is an acquaintance that she's always been attracted to, and who has a partner of her own.

Shadow's Eyes by Sydney Canyon. Tyler McCain is the owner of a large ranch that breeds and sells different types of horses. She isn't exactly thrilled when a Hollywood movie producer shows up wanting to film his latest movie on her property. Reegan Delsol is an up-and-coming actress who has everything going for her when she lands the lead role in a new film, but there one small problem that could blow the entire picture.

Light Reading: A Collection of Novellas by Sydney Canyon. Four of Sydney Canyon's novellas together in one book, including the bestsellers Shadow's Eyes and One Night.

www.ingramcontent.com/pod-product-compliance
Lightning Source LLC
LaVergne TN
LVHW091048080826
845145LV00002B/667

* 9 7 8 1 9 7 0 0 4 2 2 1 4 *